**LEABHARLANN
CHONDAE AN CHABHAIN**

1. This book may be kept three weeks.
    It is to be returned on / before the last date
    stamped below.
2. A fine of 20p will be
    or part of week a

D1513890

Don Conroy

Well known from television for his expertise on wildlife, Don is also an artist, specialising in nature illustration and cartoons, and a storyteller. He has made a particular study of the barn owl. He has written many books, among them the following:

Sky Wings

Wild Wings

The Owl Who Couldn't Give a Hoot!

The Tiger Who Was a Roaring Success!

The Bat who was all in a Flap!

The Hedgehog's Prickly Problem!

Cartoon Fun

Wildlife Fun

The Celestial Child

On Silent Wings

Don Conroy

THE O'BRIEN PRESS
DUBLIN

This revised and re-edited edition first published 1994 by The O'Brien Press
Ltd., 20 Victoria Road, Rathgar, Dublin 6, Ireland. First published 1989

British Library Cataloguing-in-publication Data
Conroy, Don
On Silent Wings
I. Title
823.914 [J]

2 4 6 8 10 9 7 5 3
96 98 00 02 04 03 01 99 97 95

Typesetting, layout, editing: The O'Brien Press Ltd.
Cover illustration: Don Conroy
Cover design: Michael O'Brien
Printing: Cox & Wyman Ltd., Reading

Author's Note

This book is the result of many years of study at several barn owl roosts in counties Kildare and Wexford. One evening, while I was watching one of these beautiful birds, it flew over to where I was hiding and sat on a bough, watching me. We looked at each other for some time, then it preened and flew away.

I promised that after such a unique encounter I would one day write about the barn owl. Then a month later a man brought me a female barn owl which had been caught in a pole trap. Both its legs were smashed, and it died on the way to the vet. That night I wrote the first chapter.

This century has seen a decline in the barn owl population over most of Europe. The reasons are not entirely clear, but the mechanisation of the agricultural industry, the destruction of hedgerows and the loss of suitable nesting sites have all certainly played their part. Widespread use of insecticides and secondary poisoning brought on by eating contaminated rodents have also contributed to the fall in numbers. In recent times farmers have tried to encourage this beneficial bird back to the farm by the erection of nesting boxes.

The countryside would be greatly impoverished by the loss of this remarkable bird, or indeed, of any of the other wonderful creatures featured in this story.

Don Conroy

For my mother Bridget and my sister Maura.

Contents

THE DAWN OF THE WORLD

Out of the great silence came the Eagle of Light,
Illuminating the skies as he flew,
And his shadow cast forth the night.
Hot airs blew from his lungs to soar upon,
The cold air to make seasons with.
Mountains to perch upon and seas to bathe in,
Lakes and rivers to drink from.
Then he imagined life and from his thought
Shattered many thoughts . . .
Trees, grasses, plants and different creatures
To live in the world.
Then he made Time.
Of all the life he created his favourite was his own,
The Birds.
They were given all the colours of the flowers
To wear upon their plumage,
Musical voices to praise him.
But above all, he gave them The Sacred Feather
And
The Gift of Flight . . .

from THE SACRED BOOK OF RAVENS

CHAPTER I

The Jaws of Death

The night was cold and clear. The silver moon shone through the faint clouds that drifted slowly by. The woods were silent and cloaked in darkness; no sound of bird or beast disturbed the quiet. Nights were getting colder, frost was sudden and severe. Wintry winds moaned through the tree tops. White hoar frost embraced the bare branches that glistened in the moonlight.

The moon was now directly above the castle, sending shafts of silvery light through every chink and window of its chambers. Long dark shadows from the castle were cast across the clearing, like some giant's hand.

A sudden shriek disturbed the silence of the night, followed by a strange hissing. Then, over the shat-

tered walls, like phantoms, flitting across the twilight, they sailed, silently gliding on soft, hushed wings.

Noctua ascended higher into the air, scanning the distant tree lines, her huge black eyes ever watchful for the slightest movement. Kos, close by, was following the exact flight path taken by his mother. The prickly frosted air made him cold despite all the extra feathers he had grown. A few short flaps, then he glided effortlessly over the leafless trees.

Kos felt good in spite of the cold – he enjoyed the freedom of the night. Only a few weeks ago he had been a downy chick, the youngest of a family of four. All he knew then was the castle walls. Now here he was, a fully-grown owl, flying in the moonlight. All the others had left the roost to make their own way in life. He knew that he, too, would have to go sometime, but he was in no hurry. He still had Noctua, always there for comfort.

He could not remember his father too well. He had not returned after hunting one night. Kos was only two weeks old at the time. Noctua seldom spoke about Hoolet, but when she did it was with great affection, for it was he who had found them their fine castle, once the home of the feared Nusham.

Over the trees, then down towards the patchwork fields quartering the ground they flew, skimming low, following the contours of the meadow, waving this way then that. Kos was finding it difficult to keep up with Noctua – yet she appeared to fly so slowly and gracefully. Sensing his effort, Noctua alighted on a hawthorn tree.

For a brief moment Kos took his eyes off her, and now she was nowhere to be seen! In a panic he circled the hedgerow and passed by the hawthorn, wondering where she had gone. Then, hearing a hiss, he flew with relief through the branches to land beside her.

'You must learn the art of concealment,' said Noctua. 'It may save your life some day.'

They both fluffed out their feathers to keep warm. Then they sat listening, and watching the meadow.

The night brewed different sounds. A fox yelped in a distant field and from the nearby farm a dog barked in annoyance. Then silence again.

'Our world is a shadowy one,' Noctua explained in

hushed tones. 'Remember it's quieter to glide than to flap. The Great Eagle has shaped us to fly silently and made our faces to transmit the smallest sound to our ears, but you need to practise and concentrate. Listen for any tell-tale rustle. It is by keen sight and sharp hearing that owls can survive and feed their family. And some day you, too, will have a family of your own.'

Kos listened, but was not thinking of a new family; he was content with life just the way it was.

'Remember too, when you do locate your prey, learn to hover over the exact spot, so you have the element of surprise. Use your feet, not your beak, to catch it. When you do catch it, you can finish it off with your beak, if it's not already dead.'

Suddenly, she heard a movement. Her head swivelled in the direction of the noise. She stared hard, then like an arrow she was gone, gliding over the fences. She hovered for a moment, then swooped down, feet forward, talons open wide. There was a squeal. Noctua spread her wings, mantling her kill, then looked around and flew back towards Kos, who by now was perched on a fence post. Before she alighted she transferred the rat to her beak, then landed alongside him. Like a baby owlet, he hissed, snorted and flapped, until the food was passed to him. He immediately gulped it down with a certain amount of difficulty, until he had only the tail to swallow –

which proved a little more awkward than he had thought. Then it was all gone.

Noctua did a little preening.

'There must be a raiding party around,' she said. 'There were two other rats where I caught him. They're probably heading for the farm.'

Kos felt a little warmer after the meal.

'Remember,' said Noctua, 'alertness, agility and patience – that's what will help you succeed in hunting. But try to avoid adult rats. They're extremely difficult to catch and if you don't get a good grip on their backs they can give you a nasty bite. An owl can be killed by the very creature it's trying to catch! When possible, stick to mice, shrews, bats or young rats.'

Kos listened attentively, watching the moonlight glisten in his mother's moist black eyes.

'It's important, too, not to waste energy on cold nights like this. We're lucky really. A mouse or rat can keep us satisfied for a long time, while other birds, who feed on grasses, have to eat nearly all the time. But, remember, food gets much scarcer in winter months. So let's see if we can stock up our larder. We can try and locate those other two rats, but you'd better let me catch them. They're a tricky lot, but worth the effort. As Hoolet often said: "One rat is worth three mice in your stomach!"'

She flew off, sailing buoyantly over the hedgerow, pausing briefly to scrutinise the ground. Kos felt the urge to cast up a pellet. He bent his head, moved from side to side, and opened and closed his mouth a few times until the pellet finally came out. It shot on to the grass. He looked to see where it had landed. There it lay, black and shining against the white frost.

He looked around for Noctua. She was further on up the field, probing the night for a meal. He could see she was 'post-hopping', one of her favourite ways to hunt – flying from post to post, pausing to check the ground, then on again.

There was still no sign of the rats. Noctua flew slowly and gently over a hedgerow, then into another field, gliding gracefully with a few wing strokes across the velvet darkness, her breast feathers blowing in the slight breeze. She continued to scan the fields, but nothing stirred. Overhead a shooting star streaked its light across the frosty midnight sky, then vanished in an instant.

Noctua began to feel cold; she wondered whether she should continue or go back to the castle where she kept a secret larder. But she knew all the signs were on for a harsh winter, when the nights would be a lot worse than this one, so she decided to persevere. Off she went, circling like a giant white moth over the ditches, then back to some more 'post-hopping', stopping to observe any movement in the long grass. Still nothing. Then away again to the last post before the next field. If that were to prove

fruitless, she decided, she might try the farmyard. That was always a good bet.

The fields were moon-drenched except for the half-shadows cast by the hedgerows. She landed on a post at the edge of the field, and SNAP! – a terrible shriek pierced the night air. Noctua crashed down below the post, wings spread out, jerking and writhing in agony. Her legs were smashed, splintered bones protruding through ripped flesh. Metal teeth tore through the ligaments. A few clouds covered the moon as if to protect it from looking down on the tragic event. Then they moved on and revealed the crimson beads of blood running down her legs over her snow-white feathers, stopping at the edge of her face, and dropping to the ground below to form a small red circle in the frost.

The shriek filled Kos with terror. He flew as fast as he could in the direction of the cry, brushing into small branches that protruded from the hedgerow. Then he saw her flapping below the post. It took him a second or two to realise fully what was happening. Noctua hung there, weak and exhausted. Kos landed on the ground, hissed, then flew up to the dreadful object which had so cruelly bitten into Noctua's legs. He kicked and pecked fiercely at the cold metal but it would not give up its vice-like grip. He shrieked and raked at it but his sharp talons were no match for this strange, vicious thing that had the jaws of death.

Exhausted, Kos stopped attacking, yet he was stricken with fear, for he could see the life ebbing away from his mother as she hung there.

Then she spoke to him. 'I'm being called by Deva, the Grey Owl, the messenger of all twilights. I have to leave, to make my silent journey. I feel my mind drifting slowly down, down, deep into the never-waking darkness . . .'

'No!' said Kos. 'Don't leave me. I'm afraid.'

'You'll be fine, don't worry,' she said feebly, trying to console him. 'You're strong and you will learn quickly. Death is something only the Nusham fear . . . For us creatures of the wild it is interwoven with our lives . . .'

Quietly she slipped away on the wings of Deva. A terrible loneliness welled up inside Kos. He sat silently watching her dead body hang there, swaying in the cold breeze that seemed to whisper the song of death. Out of the corner of his eye Kos thought he saw the shadow of an owl pass by. He swivelled his head around without moving his body but all he could see were shadows of bare branches, inked across the white field.

The night wore on. It got colder and colder. Kos fluffed up his feathers to trap some air for insulation against the icy wind, which was blowing even stronger now. He sat there quietly, anguish and pain burning inside him.

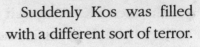

Suddenly Kos was filled with a different sort of terror. He sensed something behind him, looking at him. Slowly he twisted his body around. Amber eyes stared back at black eyes. He tried to fly but was unable to do so. With hunched shoulders he attempted to put on a threat display to ward off this creature whose eyes seemed to bore right through him. Kos was frozen with fear. Perhaps, in the deep recesses of his mind, he wanted to let it all end here with his mother.

It was a fox. It had sneaked up along the hedgerow and now stood gazing at him.

Kos tried another threat display.

The fox moved his head slightly, sniffing at the red stain below the body of Noctua. Then, looking up at Kos, he said: 'I smelt death on the wind so I came to investigate. Food is becoming scarce these nights and it will be getting worse.'

The fox was feeling extremely hungry and instinct was telling him to take the dead owl, but something else stopped him. He looked at the frozen corpse.

'It's Noctua. I knew her, you know. What a shame. Many a time our paths crossed when we were hunting. More than once she saved my hide with her loud shriek when a Nusham with the death-gun came into the field after me, and I was too busy sniffing in a hedge to notice him.'

Kos did not reply but sat bolt upright. A loud scream came from a nearby field. The fox looked away. Then a vixen came along by the ditch to join the old fox. She was carrying two rats in her mouth, which they both polished off. Kos wondered if they were the rats that Noctua had lost her life looking for.

The young vixen quickly assessed the situation. She spoke softly to Kos. 'You must go home to your roost now, little one. These bitingly cold winds can be as much a killer as the Nusham trap.'

'Farewell, white owl,' said the fox, and the two of them trotted away into the dark shadows.

Numbed with grief, Kos stayed beside the cold, damaged form that was once his mother. Night seemed to take on a brooding melancholy. Across at the farm a warm, flickering light glowed through the windows – logs were blazing on the hearth. Nusham sat laughing by the fire, unaware of the night's tragic drama.

And Kos watched Noctua sleep – the sleep of the dead.

CHAPTER II

A Rook Named Shimmer

Night slipped away over the horizon. The sky became crimson, them came streaks of yellow and blue. With the morning air the frost had retreated, apart from some patches below the hedges and at the base of the trees. A wren bobbed up and down on a bramble bush and sang a few clear notes. Blackbirds piped up, followed by a robin's melancholy song, which seemed to lament the passing of summer, or perhaps of its mate who would not return until the next breeding season.

Fieldfares and mistle thrushes were feasting on the berries of the rowan. A wood pigeon roused himself from sleep and flew over the trees. The rooks called noisily from their roost, then flew like a black cloud towards the fields, ready to exploit the new day.

Kos had kept a cold vigil beside Noctua and was still sitting there like a graven statue. He was chilled to the bone, his plumage soaked from the melting frost. The rooks spotted him.

'An owl in daytime!' exclaimed Shimmer, their leader, 'and on my favourite perch!'

'Let's teach him a lesson!' said another rook angrily.

They swooped down, cawing furiously. Kos's heart pounded with fear but he did not budge. His wings shook nervously along his body. The rooks alighted beside him on the fence.

Old Shimmer moved closer until he almost touched the owl. 'You have some nerve showing yourself in daylight, night bird. You're young, I can see it in your plumage, but that's no excuse,' he said sharply. 'Well, speak up!'

Kos did not reply, but stared at the grey pick-axe bill, knowing how capable it was of doing great damage. Then another rook interrupted.

'There's a dead owl on this post!'

Shimmer was taken completely by surprise. He hadn't noticed the body hanging from the metal trap.

'Oh, I see,' said Shimmer awkwardly. He had no love for owls but he certainly would not have wished such a horrible end as this on any creature.

'This is a cursed Nusham thing put here to trap us, or our cousins the hoodies, or even the magpies. The Nusham hate us . . .' He stopped. 'Well, I'm sorry for you, young owl.'

He looked down at the trap that had bitten deep into Noctua's legs, and remembered how he had witnessed this sorry sight before, with one of his own. He could also see the fresh scrapes and pecks made by the young owl on the metal, in the vain hope of releasing her.

'I know who it is. It's Noctua from the old castle. You must be her youngest. I haven't seen you before.' Then he added in kinder tones: 'My name is Meldeck, but my friends call me Shimmer. You needn't fear us from this day on. I'd like to be a friend, and our rookery will never harm you. You have my word on that. But beware, not all rooks will be the same, as hawks and owls are our enemies. We must leave now. Take care. We'll surely meet again.'

The rooks flew off in a clatter to a distant field.

The sky had parted with its colours and was now an overall pearly grey. Redwings called from a hawthorn, the first note of approaching winter. A hare went bounding across the field, stopped suddenly, sat up on its hind legs, ears erect, nose up sniffing the air, then went into a gallop across the field. Kos could see what had stopped the hare in its tracks; it was two Nusham. They were walking alongside the hedgerow towards him. Panic set in. Kos then remembered his mother's advice about blending into the background. Strength seemed to come into him and he darted behind some ivy that was covering a dead elm. The two Nusham stopped.

'Oh hell, you caught an owl!' exclaimed one. 'What a shame. I told you to take away that bloody trap.'

'What are you getting so het up about?' said the other. 'It's only a bloomin' bird!'

'Only a bloomin' bird? It's an owl. Very useful around the farm, they are, like a cat on wings, and there aren't many left around these parts, what's more.'

'Listen, Bill, I don't need a lecture first thing in the morning. I'm sorry about it, but you have to admit the trap has been useful for catching crows.'

'C'mon,' said Bill, 'we'd better get on with the work. We've that old tree to cut down, remember?'

'Right. But you know, that owl mightn't look half bad sitting on your mantelpiece. I could get Joe Fitz to do a nice job on it. Hide the legs behind a log and you'd have a perfect specimen.'

'Yeah?' said Bill, becoming interested.

'And you can buy me a pint tonight instead of moaning at me about the trap!' added Tom.

'Let's get that tree down first so you can earn your pint!'

The two Nusham lit their cigarettes, took the trap down from the post and walked away, the older one carrying the owl by the legs, wings outspread. They walked right past Kos and never even noticed him. His heart raced and he wanted to shriek, but he managed to stifle it. Then out through the gate went the Nusham, Kos watching as they departed with Noctua dangling beside them. All that remained of the terrible event was one broken flight feather lying on the ground below the post.

Kos looked around to make sure the coast was clear, then he flew off towards his castle. A blue tit called in alarm. Kos paused in mid-flight, shook himself to dry off his feathers, then flew on again. He felt a little better gliding over the fields with the wind blowing lightly over him. Passing the lake he could see a heron hunched over, stalking the waters.

It was a long, tiring journey back to the castle, but at last he saw it. He flapped a little harder, then glided over the wall. Two jackdaws watching from the top made a few grumbling sounds. He never even noticed them, but headed inside and over to his favourite spot on the roost.

He looked around his castle, a place of peace and safety. Shuffling about, he finally settled against the white-splashed wall, where some of his downy feathers still stuck to parts of the stone. All appeared as before – old pellets in a heap below the ledge, cobwebs hanging from the ceiling, feathers strewn around. Yet it was not the same. Alone in the empty silence, he stood ruffling his feathers and preening a little. Beside him he noticed one of Noctua's primary feathers and the whole tragedy came flooding back.

Nothing would ever be the same again. The warmth had gone from the roost. In silence he stood, thinking and staring, until finally he lulled himself to sleep.

CHAPTER III

The Coming of Emperor Fericul

In the early morning light, the gulls seemed to own the harbour, sitting high on different vessels or circling around the boats, ever-watchful for some discarded meal. They were especially partial to fish and when they saw a cormorant successfully catching one, they swooped down screaming at him, hoping he might drop it. But no fear of that, for the hungry cormorant had earned that fish and was not going to give it up to a mob of scavenging herring-gulls. He gulped it down and flew up on to a boat, spreading out his wings to dry in the cold morning air. Two gulls squabbled over a hard crust of bread on the pier.

On a bollard where a freight ship was tied up, four black and two brown rats sat, waiting anxiously. They sniffed, keeping a good look out for any Nusham.

They were a welcoming committee and they had waited for hours for the ship to arrive from foreign parts. It had docked in the early morning, but there were too many Nusham about for their visitor to make his appearance. Now that it was quiet, they knew he would show himself at any moment. They were nervous and excited, for they had never met him before, but they knew of his reputation.

Suddenly he appeared, a large fearsome-looking black rat. He was certainly bigger than any of the brown rats that were waiting – almost the size of a cat, they thought to themselves. He sniffed the air and twitched his whiskers, taking in all the information he needed about the immediate vicinity. There was a smell of Nusham, which he detested, but it was faint, a smell of fish, and an even stronger smell of rats. This pleased him.

Then he looked down and saw the waiting committee. They started to climb over each other with nervous excitement, squealing loudly as they watched him. He caught a grip of the rope and, with great agility, swung on to it. Then he walked carefully down the long rope to the pier. The other rats burst out in chorus: 'Hail, Fericul our Emperor, all hail, Fericul, our Emperor!' repeating it several times. He seemed pleased.

'Dear comrades,' he said majestically, 'it is good to be here. I have come a long way. I hope you have been expecting me?'

'Oh, yes,' said Hack,

a one-eyed rat who had lost his other eye in a fight with an alley cat. 'We've been waiting every night since we got word from your emissary of your planned visit to our shores. We've checked every ship, boat and cruiser in the harbour for the past two full moons!'

'Well done, comrades. And how is my good servant, Rattus?'

'Oh, fine, your highness,' said Hack, who had become the spokesrodent. 'He's been busy travelling around telling all the rodents in the country of your important visit.'

'A good comrade, a loyal one, and I expect his high standards from this committee. I hope that goes without saying?' A menacing look came over him.

'Oh, yes!' they replied in chorus.

'I will not tolerate any insubordination from anyone, do I make myself clear?' They all nodded and twitched their whiskers. 'Good. You will all be rewarded, I promise. Well, we cannot stay around here talking all morning. I am tired and ravenous after my journey. I trust you have some food prepared for me?'

Again Hack spoke. 'Oh, yes, fit for a king . . . I mean, fit for an emperor!'

They all smiled.

'Lead the way, my loyal comrades!' said Fericul.

Then they were off, scurrying down the long pier, sniffing and twitching as they ran across narrow streets, under parked lorries, through overgrown grass that provided excellent cover. Coming to a clearing and on to a footpath they scurried alongside the wall, always checking behind them. The wind was blowing cold, and sending old sheets of newspaper into the air.

Suddenly they saw a Nusham lying on the path up ahead. He seemed to be either asleep or dead, with a brown bottle beside him, and some old newspapers scattered about. The rats got very agitated; they wanted to go a different way.

Fericul told them to wait. He went up to sniff at the man, while the others watched him with excitement. Fericul circled the Nusham, then suddenly sank sharp yellow teeth into his hand.

Shouting with pain, the Nusham staggered to his feet, then, realising what had happened, he recoiled in horror and ran down the road, screaming and shouting in terror.

The other rats sat and watched until he was out of sight. They were as shocked as the unfortunate Nusham, but said nothing. There was now no doubt that the stories about the Emperor were true. He *had* a bloodthirsty heart. They were very glad he was on their side.

'Come on,' Fericul shouted. 'All's clear!'

Then off they went across another road, down a laneway, over a wall, and down another pathway, heading for the city dump. They stopped to drink from a small, muddy pool at the end of the lane. They sat on their hind quarters and lapped up the water with their tongues.

Fericul praised Hack on his thorough knowledge of the city.

'Oh, he's the best,' said another rat. 'He knows every hole in the wall, every gap in the hedge, every damp cellar, basement, refuse dump, all the runs along the canals, piers, and, as for getting food, he knows how to raid the best of restaurants!'

'Is that so?' said Fericul, a little annoyed at being interrupted, then he continued to lap up some more water. They moved on again, this time through a long garden, although they were a bit nervous passing over such short-cut grass.

Suddenly, from behind a bush came a large black cat with a chaffinch in its mouth. She looked as surprised as the rats were at this encounter. They stared hard at each other, tension mounting.

The cat was wondering if she might have a better meal from a rat than a half-starved bird. But could she handle all of them in a fight, she wondered?

The Emperor knew what was on the cat's mind, so he flashed his razor-sharp teeth to let her know he was ready to take her on. The other rats did the same and the cat decided not to try anything. She just walked slowly away, checking over her shoulder as she crossed the lawn.

The Emperor was seething with anger. 'If there's one thing I hate more than hawks and owls, it's bloody cats! Come on, let's get out of here,' and away they went.

Finally they approached the dump. The icy winds brought the smells they liked, and, sneaking through a gap in the fence, they were soon back on a familiar path where they all felt more relaxed. Herring and black-headed gulls were circling overhead, and the rats ignored them. They scurried under broken furniture, over an old mattress, across damp newspapers, past a rusty fridge, until they reached a tunnel that went underground. It was really an old, cracked water-pipe, half-submerged in all the rubbish. It had proved to be an excellent home, and most of the clay had been excavated to make a large, warm dwelling-place below ground.

The Emperor seemed pleased. He took a deep sniff and twitched his whiskers. Twenty rats came from below to greet him, including Rattus, who was nearly as large as Fericul.

They made a circle around Fericul and chanted his praises. Then they all went below out of the cold winds. There, Hack revealed a most bountiful larder.

Fericul's eyes gleamed as he began to gorge himself. They all joined in, and there was plenty to eat. Rattus had already tested the food, for he was the Emperor's official taster. There was no way that rats would eat putrid food, unlike stupid dogs! They tore at the carcass of a chicken – Fericul even polished off some bones – then bacon, apples, cheese, bread and a cherry pie. Fericul praised his followers for the feast and assured them that they would be rewarded. They did not know what the reward would be, but they were delighted to hear it.

Six rats came and groomed the Emperor. He sat squatting, enjoying every moment.

The other rats all lay around, full to the whiskers. Fericul, in a more serious mood, continued: 'I want to meet all my followers from the city and the surrounding areas tonight.'

'That will be difficult. It takes a lot of organising at such short notice,' said Spike, a brown rat with an extra-long fang.

The Emperor just glared at him, then spoke in menacing tones. 'I hope I make myself clear. I said TONIGHT! Is that understood?'

'Oh, yes . . . of course,' said Spike, quivering with fear. 'It will be organised right now.'

Then Rattus, Hack, Thrasher and Spike bowed down in front of the Emperor. They were about to leave when Fericul spoke to Hack.

'Well done for supplying the excellent food today.'

'I'll gladly provide the food again for tonight's banquet,' Hack said with pride. 'There's a restaurant nearby where they fill large black bags with tasty meals of the finest quality. I can confidently guarantee enough food for all!'

'Oh, clever Hack,' said Fericul. 'From now on you will be my official spokesrodent!'

'This is indeed a great honour,' said Hack. 'I'll raid every restaurant, store house, shop and orchard to see that you're well catered for during your stay. This is my solemn pledge.'

Fericul patted him on the back. 'Now your Emperor will rest. Off with you. We will meet again at twilight. Convey my desires to all my comrades.'

They bowed down before him again and left, some of them first making a bed of feathers for the Emperor. He lay down, stretched a little, belched, yawned, and then slept soundly.

*　　*　　*

Icy winds blew over the city. Lights came on in the houses. As the moon hung low in the sky, Nusham journeyed home from their offices and work places. All Nusham activity was gone from the dump for another day. The evening now belonged to the rats. An uneasy silence hung over the place.

Then out they came, black-furred bodies in their thousands, from dark, damp hiding-places, like a vast army on manoeuvres, heading for the dump. They were soon joined by mice from all the nearby houses.

The rats were very excited, as this was the first time they would set eyes on their leader. Some had even thought he was only a legend. The mice and shrews were excited just being there, although they always felt uncomfortable when rats were about, because rats had such a confident and arrogant demeanour.

They entered the dump through the gap in the fence, bobbing up and down, scrambling over each other, twitching, squealing, panting, sniffing. It was as if a sea of rodents was moving over the rubbish. The older rats used the runs, that were marked by Hack with urine and droppings, to get ahead of the younger ones. Then they sat squatting on the rubble at the mouth of the tunnel, an enormous gathering, waiting in frenzied anticipation, with stiffened fur and scaly tails wriggling. There were even a few bank-voles there that had travelled a long way just to be present at such an important occasion.

The rats had all the best positions, rows and rows of them sitting, with claws splayed like talons, and pushing away mice or shrews who might dare try to usurp their positions. The more pushy rats were at the front – these were usually the sewer rats.

Hack appeared up the tunnel first. A surge of excitement greeted him – all eyes watching, the hubbub of voices rising and falling. He looked around at the huge collection of rodents, and, knowing that he hadn't managed to invite a quarter of them, he was delighted at such a big turn-out. He would have been just as glad if those wimps, the mice, had stayed at home, and as for the shrews with their high-pitched squeals, they had better be quiet and just listen. And how did those dopes, the bank-voles, hear about it? Still, it made an impressive crowd.

'My dear comrades, you are all most welcome here this evening on this most auspicious occasion,' he began. 'Tonight we are proud to have with us our great leader, who has journeyed a very long way just to be here among us, to share with us his great wisdom and his plans for our future. He is the one who can save all animals from extinction.

'Our beloved leader has come to give one of his rare public appearances. It's the night we've all been waiting for. I won't delay the proceedings any longer except to say that our beloved Emperor has invited you all to stay for refreshments after the speech.'

Loud cheers came from the crowd.

'And now I would like to call on our great leader – Emperor Fericul. Let's give him a rousing rodent welcome!'

The crowds were ecstatic, the cheers and squeals rang through the cold night air.

'Silence!' shouted Hack.

Then the Emperor appeared from below, his paws outstretched.

'My brothers and sisters, it is good to be here.' More loud cheers. 'I have travelled to nearly every corner of the world. How did I do this? By my own skill, strength and, above all, ingenuity. I use my ingenuity

to tap Nusham ingenuity. They build boats and ships; I travel in them! They make food; I eat it! Our forefathers knew how to tolerate Nusham by exploiting their abilities. The Nusham has ability, you must agree, comrades. Who made this haven for us? Nusham! They are our slaves. They don't know it yet, but some day they will. Nusham will bow down to me and to all of you, I promise!'

The rats banged their feet, hissing and squealing with delight.

Meanwhile Hack, Spike, Thrasher and Rattus kept a keen look-out for any intruders like Nusham, dogs, cats, or even an owl, who might be foolish enough to disturb the proceedings.

Moving closer to the crowd, Fericul continued: 'But we cannot afford to be too complacent about Nusham, for they have a loathing for us. We have been frozen, heated, burned, decapitated, given electric shocks, injected, drowned, drugged and even eaten by them. They have made sport at our expense, even thrown our brothers into a pit with terrier dogs, who slaughtered every last one of them.'

All eyes fastened on to his. His words sent shivers down their spines.

'That's what we are dealing with, my comrades – vile creatures!'

The crowds were stunned and such hatred was aroused that they were prepared to take on every

Nusham and tear out their savage hearts.

'They secretly envy us, you know,' he continued with a sinister smile. 'They copy our runs, which they call roads! Some even live and work below ground. I myself have heard them refer to their race not as the Nusham race, nor an owl nor cat race, but, comrades, a rat race!'

The crowds were amazed.

'Even in the days of the great Nusham "hate wars", they made large rat-like runs all across the countryside. In fact they killed so many of their own kind that the rats were convinced there could be no more Nusham. Rats dined handsomely on their dead soldiers in those days. But, somehow, some of them managed to survive. Even in the golden age of rodents, when our forefathers carried the killer fleas on their backs and almost destroyed the entire Nusham race, they still managed to survive. But when I'm through, comrades, there will be no more Nusham except the ones I choose as my slaves. And as for those other pests – owls, hawks and the like – I will destroy all of them. I have started already, my comrades. Have you not noticed? I have cursed the great elm with disease. The owls and hawks will soon have no place to rest, and if they have no place to rest or roost they will not survive!'

Great cheers rose from the crowds. The mice and shrews certainly had noticed a lot of elm trees being

cut down by the Nusham because of a strange disease. The Emperor had, without doubt, great magical powers, they thought to themselves.

'Well, my comrades, it is late and I know you must all be feeling cold and hungry. It is time for the feast. You are all welcome to share it with me. And soon we will meet again, when I will be able to give you all a special gift!'

There were squeals and squeaks, tapping and clapping for their beloved Emperor.

'Now it is time to dine,' said Fericul. 'I am so hungry I could eat a Nusham!'

They all hurried to a discarded van where the food was stored. They gorged themselves and told tales of cunning and victory over the Nusham, and over cats, dogs, falcons, owls, horses and hawks, cursing all who were not rodents. And then they slept.

The mice, shrews and voles did not manage to get into the feast because of the rats. So they headed home feeling very cold, but in awe of their great leader, and they wondered when they would meet him again and what the 'special gift' would be.

CHAPTER IV

Going It Alone

Moonlight peeped through the window into the ruined castle where Kos was sleeping. Slowly he awoke, then looked around, expecting to see his mother waiting for him, ready to set off for a night's foray. Then all too quickly he realised that this would never happen again. A wave of grief engulfed him.

His life was totally changed. He would no longer live in a cocoon of security; the world would be a different place now. He was frightened. Then the spirit of Noctua seemed to whisper comforting thoughts to him, so he roused himself, shook off the drowsiness from his body and flew out of the roost to perch on the castle wall.

Bobbing his head from side to side to scan the ground below the castle, he gave a loud shriek that

echoed through the still night. He preened himself meticulously, checking every feather, and spreading oil from his oil gland on to his feathers with his bill. Then he wiped his bill on the stone wall. A quick shuffle of his wings, then he stretched them one at a time. He felt good, but very hungry.

He listened for any sounds with his acute hearing, but all seemed quiet. It was late, later than usual. Noctua would have been ready to hunt at dusk. Then another thought bothered him, the thought of Hoolet, his father, not returning after a night's hunting. This made him tense. It was a dangerous world out there. If only his brother Driad were here, but he had left two weeks earlier to make his own way in life. Kos hoped he was all right, wherever he was.

Kos did not relish the idea of hunting alone, but sooner or later he would have to do it.

46

It was a bright, starry night. The moon had a pale ring around it and in the distance he could see heavy clouds moving across the sky. A cold breeze ruffled his feathers, then he launched himself into a decisive glide over the treetops. He felt more relaxed now; there was nothing better than to ride the air in utter silence.

The trees were awash with a silver light. Down through the dark woods he went, flitting in and out like a white ghost. He was not hunting as much as exploring, flying low over the ground, then high over the trees and out over the fields. He felt pleased that he could fly past a group of rabbits so silently that they did not even notice him. Then he alighted on a tall, gnarled oak tree and simply sat and watched. He could see two horses standing very still in a nearby field. He saw yellow lights glowing from the farm house. It looked friendly, yet he knew it was the home of the Nusham.

There was movement below the oak. A strange-looking nocturnal creature had come through a gap in the hedge, grubbing for worms near the exposed roots. Kos was fascinated, for he had never seen a badger before. Later he would get to know old Bawson, but for the moment he was simply curious, and very cautious. The badger looked up once, then continued to dig. He did not seem to be having any luck, for, despite all the digging, Kos didn't see him

eat anything. He gave up after a time and plodded off, nose to the ground, towards the midnight woods, his body brushing the ground as he moved.

Then there was silence again. Kos looked up at the clouds overhead and remembered Noctua's words about getting to know the signs for bad weather. He stared hard, wondering about these clouds; then he noticed the myriad specks of white drifting slowly down from the darkness, beautiful white flakes that almost mesmerised him. One went into his eye and made him blink. He was enchanted, for snow was another thing he had never seen before. He opened his mouth to catch some, and repeated this a number of times until the inside of his mouth felt cold.

He amused himself with another trick. If he stayed very still and let the snowflakes gather upon his head, he could then bend over, swivel his head and shake them off. He was really enjoying this until his feathers became damp and he felt cold. Then off he went on hushed wings again, this time to do some hunting, as his stomach felt hollow and empty.

Flying about hedge-high and watching the inky shadows made by the trees and hedges, Kos wondered how it was that the shadows were longer than the trees themselves. Flap, flap, flap, then he relaxed into a long glide, scanning the ground. He knew how important it was to get to know his area. Noctua had known every tree, hedge, gateway, post and gap in the vicinity. Well, it was up to him to be just as good, if not better.

A cold chill came into his heart every time he thought of Noctua. He forced himself to banish the vision of her lying below that post with her legs broken, and began instead to think of warm and satisfying memories, like when he was an owlet watching and waiting for her to return to the nest. She always gave that little liquid shriek to let him know she was arriving home. Then she would appear at the window with a tasty morsel in her bill, look once over her shoulder, and fly to him. He would take the food and bolt it down, then they would sleep, touching against each other. This made him feel calm and happy and serene.

He was so lost in pleasant thoughts that he hadn't

noticed how heavily the snow had been falling. It had a sort of hypnotic effect. He found it hard to focus yet he continued to fly, the lights from the farmhouse helping him to get his bearings. Noctua had said that there was particularly good hunting near farmyards, for all Nusham farms attract rats and mice. As he got closer the lights from the house alarmed him, for he could see the silhouettes of the Nusham passing backwards and forwards inside. He was fraught with anxiety and yet had a great curiosity to see again the Nusham who had taken away the body of Noctua.

Alighting on the window sill he peered in. A warm fire glowed red and orange, with an occasional blue flicker breaking through the burning peat. One Nusham sat on a sofa, looking into the fire and sucking on his pipe. A dog lay close to the warm hearth, his body twitching as he dreamed his dream of chasing rabbits over the fields.

Four Nusham were sitting around a table, playing cards and talking loudly. A large female Nusham came through the door carrying a hot supper. She shook the shoulder of the Nusham sitting on the couch. A younger Nusham entered the room with a tray of sandwiches and danced around the table before plonking them down in the middle of the game. There were shouts of laughter, and all of them were totally unaware that from outside on the cold sill they were being watched by a very curious owl.

While Kos observed the goings-on inside the house, a pair of green eyes watched from the barn the dark shape of the owl on the sill. Then the farm cat moved quietly out through the shadows until she was directly below Kos.

'*Miaow, miaow*, white owl, what are you doing here? Are you lost? Do you want shelter? Maybe you're hungry? Yes, that must be the reason you came out on such a cold night.

'I can help you. It's warm in the barn and there are lots of mice. I caught one earlier today. In fact, it's still there; I have no need of it because I'm well fed by the Nusham. But you must be hungry. Come and eat up.

'Look, the barn's just over here. Hurry, before anyone sees you through the window.'

Kos wondered how the cat knew he was hungry. She certainly seemed friendly, yet he remembered Noctua warning him about cats – or was it dogs, or both? Well, there could be no harm in looking. He watched the cat skulk in and out of the shadows and across the snow, then squeeze through the great wooden doors that were partly open. Kos followed. He landed on the ground at the doors and looked into the barn to check that the cat was not lying in ambush. Then he saw her walking on top of some bales of hay.

'Come on in,' she called. 'There's nothing to be afraid of . . . it's over here.'

Kos flew in and circled around the barn. There was plenty of farm machinery there, and bales of hay that reached up to the rafters.

Kos sat on the rafters looking around and watching the cat from a safe distance. The cat beckoned him down to take the mouse. Kos didn't move, just stared.

'Do you want the mouse or not?' said the cat. 'I'm not going to hand-feed you! If you want it, it's just in the corner below that bale of hay . . .'

Kos couldn't see any mouse from where he was.

The cat stretched herself out on the bale and played with the straw as if she were a kitten. Deciding to chance it, Kos swooped down and landed near her. The cat immediately pulled herself into an upright sitting position.

'Go on, get it! I'll keep guard.'

Swivelling his head, Kos looked over his shoulder behind the bale, but still he could not see anything, so he jumped down to search for his gift. It was nowhere to be found. He was about to ask where it was when he saw the cat change from a friendly creature into a snarling, hissing bundle of trouble.

'Well, you *are* the foolish owl, aren't you?'

The paws were now claws, and fangs were showing through a half-smile. The green eyes were half-closed and menacing, the ears flattened back behind the head, as the cat prepared to lunge forward and make a meal out of him. Kos's eyes darted around the barn in terror, his head bobbing back and forth. He was shaking with fear. He was trapped! He had to make a split-second decision: would he try and fly past the cat who stood between two large bales of hay, or would he throw himself on his back and hope he could hold her off with his talons?

Suddenly a Nusham called. 'Muffet, Muffet, where are you? Here kitty, kitty, kitty!'

It was enough to distract the cat. Kos seized his opportunity, and flew over the cat towards the rafters. She sprang up like a leopard, seething and clawing at fresh air, for Kos was out of reach and on the rafters in a flash. The cat fell backwards on to the bales of hay, furious at having missed her chance.

'Muffet, are you in there?' said a voice from the barn doors.

The cat sprang down and hurried towards the exit. 'I'll get you later,' she snarled. 'You can't escape, white owl!' Then she left.

Kos flew towards the window above the doors, and

watched the Nusham pick up the cat.

'You naughty puss, making me come out for you on this cold night!'

The cat miaowed and purred. The Nusham put the cat on her shoulder and went towards the house. The cat stared hard over the shoulder at the barn, her eyes still menacing. She watched Kos stare back in triumph. The door of the house opened and a flood of golden light spread on the ground, casting long shadows of the Nusham and the cat. Then it closed. The cat was gone at last.

Kos waited until things were quiet again, then he made his way out through the broken window. He faced into the wind and off he flew with a delicious feeling of freedom, over a belt of trees, then out across the patchwork fields, winging his way home. The snow had stopped falling, and everything was shrouded in white. Everywhere looked so bright, the snow coating the winter-bare trees and lying along the hedges. Kos dipped and dived, swooped and glided; he was in his element, the light breeze on his face, the wind rushing through his feathers.

Looking across the fields, the world seemed timeless as he flew through the deepest hours of night. He somehow felt invincible. Maybe it was because he had survived all the things that had happened to him. He could still see Noctua vividly in his imagination flying alongside him. He thought that if he didn't have

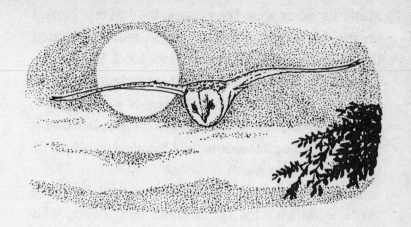

her actual presence, he would always have her in his mind. This brought him great comfort.

Beyond some more trees the castle loomed up out of the darkness. With a burst of energy he sped back to his roost. He glided over the wall and in through a small window to the inner room, which was dark and secure, just the way he liked it. Settling himself against the wall, he tucked one leg into his body feathers, and slowly eased himself into sleep.

* * *

The next couple of days brought more snow. The trees were heavy with it. The branches at times became so laden that they bent under the weight, and sometimes even broke and came crashing down to end up in a mound of snow at the base of the tree.

Mistle thrushes were busy eating the last few berries on the holly tree, while all the tit families banded together and combed the woods for food. Blue, great, coal and long-tailed tits would systematically move from one tree to the next, sometimes joined by the chaffinches in their search. Roosting early, because it was dark by late afternoon, the blue tits would huddle together to keep warm.

There was a thick covering of ice on the lake which made it difficult for the mallards and coots, who slipped and skated on the surface. A solitary heron stood by the lake on one leg to keep the heat in. Mute swans were joined by their winter relations, the bewick and whooper swans. They seemed to be having more success feeding in the fields on the frosty grasses. Lapwings tumbled from the sky to join the swans. The north wind cut like a knife and many young birds died during the night from the severe air frost. The whole countryside was locked in the grip of a hard, cold winter.

Kos had not ventured out for several days. He remembered the secret larder that Noctua had hidden for emergencies and polished it off. He spent a great deal of time looking out on the wintry landscape. He enjoyed seeing the things which he would normally have missed while sleeping.

He finally decided to set out hunting again, driven

by the pangs of hunger. There was a hushed silence all around. It was still bright, being early afternoon, too bright for an owl, but all he wanted now was food. A cold biting wind blew, making him reluctant to leave the warmth of his castle. Yet he knew that once he was airborne he would be fine. He flew out on to the castle wall and looked around. Nothing seemed to be moving, except him. Then off he went, flying over the frozen fields in silence. Although the snow had stopped, there were snow-drifts everywhere, blocking trails and creeping up the tree trunks and the walls of the castle.

Kos circled the whole area, then landed on a telegraph pole. A large flock of starlings flew above him, making interesting shapes as they passed, like a ball at first, then like a long streak, then back to a ball shape. More and more flocks joined them, giving a most spectacular display. Kos had never seen anything like it before. There seemed to be thousands of birds all swirling in unison across the grey sky. Craning his neck too far back to view the spectacle, he nearly fell off the post.

This was the testing month for all creatures young and old. Many would perish from the severity of the weather. Nature seemed suspended, as if held prisoner by some enchanted spell that would never be broken. Hardly a leaf or sprig of green showed through the blanket of snow. The heavy blue-grey

skies promised more snowfalls.

As Kos sat in chilled solitude, something moved in a distant field. Quickly focusing his attention on it, he could clearly see something reddish-brown against the snow.

With a rush of wings he soared high, planning to make a surprise attack. Maybe this was a meal at last! A jay, scratching for something to eat at the edge of the woods, called in alarm. Kos watched as it shot into the trees. The wary jay sat still, crown erect, flicking his tail in annoyance, as he watched the owl mount the air and pass overhead.

Kos hoped the harsh, shrill cry of the jay hadn't disturbed what he was after. No, he could still see it picking away near the hedgerow. When Kos was directly above, he hovered, then dropped like a stone with talons outstretched. He had never dropped from so high a point and as he plummeted down he suddenly realised that the creature was a lot bigger than he had first imagined. Trying to stop his dive-bomb in mid-flight proved not to be as easy as he had hoped. Too late, he crashed on to a cock pheasant. Instinctively he knew that he had made a mistake in tackling this large bird.

The pheasant let out a loud hiss, and in an instant had shaken Kos from his back, spun around, and landed a well-aimed kick into the owl's stomach. Kos was flung through the air and he landed on his back with his wings spread out. A sharp stab of pain coursed through his body. He was dazed and winded.

When he could focus properly again he saw the pheasant's red face glaring down on him. The cock held Kos down with one foot and was ready to strike with the other.

The pheasant hissed. 'Are you crazy, owl? Did you really think you could tackle me? I've a good mind to finish you off with my spur!'

Kos did not reply. He couldn't – he felt as if his stomach was punctured.

Suddenly, the pheasant flew away over the hedge-row in a great hurry. A little surprised, but greatly relieved, Kos sat up, feeling sore and dizzy. He shook both wings to remove the powdered snow from his feathers. A shadow passed over him and looking quickly around he saw his old friend the fox staring back at him.

'We meet again!' said the fox.

Kos now realised why the pheasant had taken flight.

'Well, you made me miss my supper, and it was such a tasty-looking pheasant,' sighed the old fox. 'Don't tell me you were trying to catch it yourself?' he continued, looking reproachfully at Kos.

Kos nodded, feeling rather foolish.

'You'll need to learn a lot more woodcraft if you're

to survive around here, young fellow. By the way, I'm called Crag. I'm the oldest fox in these parts, an honour I didn't attain by taking foolish risks. So you had better take heed. What are you called?'

'Kos,' replied the owl.

'You must be as ravenous as I am, so let's try and find some food.'

Crag trotted off along the hedge followed overhead by Kos, who kept at a safe distance.

They had reached the edge of the woods when Crag noticed something and started to sniff it. It was cow dung. Crag began to move it about with his nose.

'You're not going to eat that?' exclaimed Kos.

Crag turned it over to reveal two beetles and a worm, which he quickly gobbled up. Then he started to roll over in it. Kos didn't know what was going on. He wondered if the fox had taken leave of his senses.

Crag continued to roll about in the dung for a couple of minutes. 'That should conceal my scent. I used to do that to get the hounds off my trail, and it worked!'

Kos didn't know what he was talking about, but it sounded interesting. He was also impressed by the way the fox could melt into the shadows and then reappear through the dense undergrowth. Kos flitted in and out among the trees. The night was upon them, but there was still no sign of food.

Crag sniffed the wind. 'Let's go to the river, there

are always a few river rats lurking about!'

Venturing forward, they crept like silent shadows against the white fields towards the river. They moved along the hedgerows until they came to a ditch near the river's edge. Two lights could be seen in the distance.

'Don't move,' said Crag.

Cautiously, Kos dropped down beside him. They watched the lights curve into the darkness.

'We'll just wait until it goes past.'

A car roared past them, then came to a sudden halt further up the road. As they watched, a black bag was thrown from it. It rolled down the bank and stopped near the water's edge. The car then sped away into the night.

'We're in luck,' said Crag. 'That bag should bring out the rats. I'll wait down there behind that tree stump; you go over to the willow.' Taking up positions, they waited.

The waiting made Kos very nervous. Suppose they were adult rats, could he handle them? He recalled his mother's warning. Then they came, four rats at first, followed by two more. They sniffed nervously, but must not have noticed Crag's scent, for they started to pick a hole through the bag until its contents spilled out onto the river bank – bottles, cans, cartons, wrappers, then success! Food – slices of bread and a chicken leg! One rat went into the bag and came out

with a string of sausages. Another started pulling at them while the rest polished off the bread. Kos and Crag sprang to the attack. Swooping down from the willow, Kos killed a rat instantly. Crag leaped into the middle of the rats, jaws snapping, but all he got was a rat's tail as they scurried to safety. Kos mantled his kill and was about to enjoy it, but he noticed that Crag had missed the other rats. He dropped his meal, flew after them, and found one about to leap into the river. Swinging his legs forward he snatched the rat with his sharp talons. The rat twisted round and bit deeply into Kos's leg.

Ignoring the bite, Kos killed the rat with his beak and carried it back to the fox.

'Your meal,' he said.

Crag looked pleased, and quickly gulped it down. Kos picked up his rat and bolted it down too. They both enjoyed their long-awaited meal. Crag could have eaten ten of them.

'You did very well, my little friend. You've proved yourself tonight. You'll make out all right!'

Kos felt satisfied and pleased with himself. They sat for a long time looking at the trees framed against the starry sky.

'Well, I'd better get back to Asrai,' said Crag at last. 'She gets very broody at this time of year and I don't want any frisky young fox sniffing about her. If you need me at any time, I live at the edge of the woods beside the old oak that was struck by lightning. My earth is part of old Bawson's sett. Farewell for now.' The fox loped away.

Kos gave a small shriek and flew high over the treetops, the branches glistening in the moonlight as he passed above. He could see the great elms standing like guards at each corner of the field. On he sailed, his wings beating slowly, his beak carving a way through the frosty air. Proud thoughts filled his mind. Here he was, flying well and now a skilled hunter able to provide for himself and his new friend, Crag.

Then another thought quickly dispelled his pride. The fox had had to rescue him from a very angry pheasant. He was in danger there. He wondered how long it would take him to learn to survive? His leg began to throb with pain from the rat's bite, and his stomach was feeling sore from the kick he had got from the pheasant. He would be glad to get home.

Then he saw the castle up ahead. Coming down to perch on the wall for a few moments, he looked around. Faint hoots could be heard from nearby conifers. He was tempted to investigate, but decided against it and flew into his roost. Carefully tucking his injured leg into his body feathers, he fluffed himself. His last thoughts were of Crag, hoping he had reached home safely. Of course he would have. He was a resourceful old fox. Then, slowly but surely, Kos sank down into a deep sleep.

CHAPTER V

The Shooting Party

The tranquil morning was shattered by the sound of gunfire. Blackbirds called in alarm. Jays went screaming through the woods. The rooks rose like a great black cloud from their rookery and circled in the sky.

Kos was jolted from his slumber. He sensed that something terrible was going on. Shivering with fright, his heart pounding in his body, he inched his way over to the window and peered out cautiously. There was a tremendous commotion. Gunfire pierced the peaceful woods. Dogs barked. Kos could sense a wave of terror from all the creatures – then, an unearthly silence.

Kos wasn't sure whether he should fly away or stay still. He could hear the tramping of Nusham feet through the woods, getting closer and closer. Then a soothing voice called. It was Crag.

'Keep out of sight, Kos. The Nusham will be passing into the fields behind the castle shortly. It'll be dangerous to be seen.'

Crag found a way into the castle through a broken wall and came up the spiral stairs until he was in the chamber which Kos used as a roost.

'Are they coming to get us all?'

'No,' said Crag, 'it's the pheasants they're after. They won't stop until they get as many as they can. But we must keep quiet. If the dogs get my scent they'll be in here after us.'

The wait was agonisingly long, the footfall menacing, as it crunched nearer and nearer. Then the Nusham and their dogs passed by the castle. Kos's stomach fluttered with nerves as he heard the Nusham talking and laughing. Then silence again. Crag stole a glance out the window.

'They're gone,' he said, with a sigh of relief.

They both relaxed a little.

'This could go on for weeks,' added Crag. 'But at least they don't shoot at night!'

'Why this sudden attack on pheasants?' asked Kos anxiously.

'Well, it's difficult to explain, really. They hate us foxes, I know, but they give the impression that they really like pheasants. It's very puzzling. I've often seen the Nusham caring for young pheasants and feeding them in special pens. Yet the strange thing is, later on they release them. First, they're set free and then there's this onslaught on them. They shoot every one of them!'

'Maybe the pheasants upset the Nusham in some way that makes them angry?' suggested Kos.

'I don't think so. Pheasants are harmless. I know the Nusham hunt me because sometimes, when I'm really hungry, I take one of their hens. But pheasants don't do anything to anyone. I tell you, Kos, Nusham are impossible to fathom.'

The afternoon brought back a serenity to the fields and woods. The dreaded smell of the Nusham lingered in the air for a long time and their footprints could be seen everywhere. Red tubes of spent cartridges were strewn about on the ground.

CHAPTER VI

Telling Tales

The Emperor Fericul had settled into his new home at the rubbish tip. Hack, Spike, Thrasher and Rattus were at his side constantly. They watched him stuff himself with food every day and they fulfilled all his demands and whims.

One morning he called a meeting of the committee.

'You know why I'm here, don't you?' They all nodded, not really sure. 'I have found where the ancient secret site is!' They looked blank. 'You know about the temple of claw, spoken of in legends and tales? Well, my comrades, after much searching and questing, I have finally located it, and it is on this very island!' They all looked suitably pleased.

'It lies below an ancient Nusham burial site, and I know the exact place!' His voice quivered with excitement. 'I have discovered RATLAND! Yes, Ratland, the home of the ancient ones!'

Breaking into monstrous laughter, Fericul stopped and looked at them with an evil grin. 'Are you not pleased, my comrades?'

They all burst into spontaneous hurrahs.

'Good, good, my comrades. Finding Ratland is only the beginning. We will truly be masters of this earth very shortly!' They all applauded.

'Tell all rodents the news, and very soon we shall meet in Ratland, where rats and their kin will know that I am the Chosen One. All other creatures will come to know it too. Now, I want to be alone.' Fericul retired to rest again.

The committee of rats departed. They found some food to eat and sat in one of the chambers. Rattus was feeling very relaxed, and he spoke to the others as he had never spoken before.

'I'm glad to see the Emperor happy. I've never seen him so content and pleased with things. You know, of course, that he's not a *true* emperor. He doesn't come from any royal line, if you know what I mean. He's not even a rat in the true sense of the word. Neither am I, if it comes to that. We're two of a kind. We began our lives in glass cases. *We were made by the Nusham!*'

The other rats' jaws dropped open. They couldn't believe their ears.

'Yes,' he continued. 'We two are a mixture of the black and brown rat, with a little bit of coypu thrown in. That's what gives us this unusual size. And we're rather cunning too!' He smiled, flashing his yellow incisors. 'I suppose you could call us laboratory escapees, or freaks!' He laughed loudly.

'You don't understand? Well, the Nusham have been experimenting with us rodents for a long time. They like neither our temperament nor our colour, so they produce milky-white docile rats that will do any number of tricks for a morsel of food. It's pathetic, really. They keep these rats in glass cases – and not only rodents, I've seen snakes, monkeys, dogs, spiders, lizards and even small Nusham in these glass cases.

'Then, for some special reason we'll never know about, the Nusham bred me and Fericul, large and black and strong. We were kept in the cases too. Well, we got so fed up being handled, and poked and punctured with long needles, that we decided to escape.

'I remember it well. There was a violent storm raging one evening when Fericul and I planned our escape. We knew that each evening there would be only one Nusham on guard in the laboratory. Fericul pretended to be having a seizure. He began to shake and squeal, waving his tail nervously. He was anything but nervous. I was, but he was fearless.

'Well, the Nusham came over to investigate, and Fericul played dead, his eyes glazed. He was so convincing that the Nusham gently lifted him out and placed him on a ledge in order to feel the heartbeat. Fericul seized his opportunity, and lunged straight for the Nusham's throat! A scream came from the unfortunate Nusham as he tried to free himself from the deadly grip. I remember him crashing to the ground, knocking glass cases and cages as he fell. The creatures in the cases were unhurt and began scurrying about. A tarantula climbed up the wall and a monkey hopped about in a frenzy of excitement, knocking down everything in his path. Fericul did not let go until he was sure the Nusham was lifeless. Then there was a strange silence. Fericul looked up at me with a demonic stare in his eyes. "Well, it worked. Let's go!"

'But I was still trapped in my glass case. Fericul had an idea and started to climb up to the monkey who

was busy hurling objects to the floor. He sneaked up behind him and sank his teeth into the monkey's arm. The monkey screamed with pain and anger, and raced across the ledge, knocking every glass case to the floor, including mine. I suddenly found myself free. "Come on!" Fericul shouted. We got through the first door, as it was partly open. Behind us we left a trail of broken objects and shattered glass and terrified creatures scrambling for cover. The Nusham lay silent on the floor. We gnawed our way through the other door to freedom, then out into the night air. The winds raged and the rain beat down upon us.

'We moved cautiously along the wide streets, dazzling lights flashing different colours at us. This was our first time out in the real world. But we had stealth and cunning and we knew that if we could survive a world of Nusham we could live anywhere, and we did. We got food from a nearby restaurant and slept in a warm pipe . . .'

The other rats looked terrified as they listened to his story.

'There's no need to look so alarmed,' added Rattus. 'We're all friends here, and everything I said is true. The Emperor is just a name he uses. He feels he's destined for great things, and, who knows, he probably is!'

A long shadow fell across the faces of the listeners, for behind Rattus stood Fericul. Rattus turned around nervously. 'D . . . did you have a good rest? I was just telling them about our escape from the N . . . Nusham laboratory.'

'Leave us!' roared Fericul to the other rats.

They quickly scurried into another chamber, shivering with fright.

'Do you think the Emperor heard what Rattus was saying?' asked Spike.

'I don't think he looked too pleased!'

There was a terrible scream from the other chamber. The rats were seized with fear.

'Do you think he's . . . killed Rattus?' Spike wondered nervously.

Fericul appeared out from the chamber, and all eyes stared. He flashed his yellow teeth – they were covered in blood. 'Is there no one I can trust? My First-In-Command talking deceit! Lies, lies, all lies.

And I suppose you believed him?'

'No!' they all replied.

'He had a lust for power. A cunning adversary, wanting to usurp my position because I had discovered Ratland. That's the thanks I get! He dared call me a freak because *he* wanted to be ruler. Well, there is only one ruler, one emperor! Am I right?'

'There is only one emperor and his name is Fericul, our true leader!' they all shouted, repeating this several times. All the rats around heard them and joined in the chorus.

'I am the ruler of the under-earth and will soon be supreme ruler over all the earth!' proclaimed Fericul.

They all cheered again. 'Hail, Fericul, the ruler of the under-earth and soon to be the supreme lord over all the earth!'

CHAPTER VII

The Prisoner

Weeks passed, winter persisted, and there were more heavy snowfalls over the countryside. A hush of white muffled any sounds around. Night brought cold, piercing winds that moaned across the countryside, chilling the life out of many a wren and goldcrest. Kos listened to the wind whining through the empty corridors of the castle; he went out now only for brief periods in the early mornings and at twilight. Food was scarce.

Early one morning he awoke to the song of a mistle thrush singing from a yew tree. Then he noticed a band of tits flying with some chaffinches to distant fields. Kos watched them and wondered where they were going. He had seen them do this several times before, and this time he decided to investigate. He

knew they must be searching for food, for that was the one thing that would drive them out of the woods. His own hunger pangs and curiosity were what drove him.

The winter-bare trees stood stark against the sky as Kos flew towards the frozen fields. The wind ruffled his feathers as he flapped and glided hedge-high over the ground, his thoughts drifting between the past and the present as he remembered the comforting way Noctua would nuzzle the nape of his neck with her beak. He felt a glow just thinking about it. The grief was less sharp now compared to the first throbbing pains of loss that had pulled at his mind. It was Noctua's own words that rang in his head: 'Time is a great healer', and it was true now for Kos.

Still following the band of birds up ahead, he kept

a safe distance so as not to alarm them, yet remained on course; rumbles came from his hollow stomach to remind him of the real reason for his pursuit. He picked up speed – a few quick flaps – then glided again. He was near the farm now, and feeling very wary after his last visit there.

But the birds did not stop at the farm. They continued on for quite a long time until they reached row upon row of houses. They headed for the gardens at the back, and there Kos saw many small tables with bread and nuts for these very hungry visitors. He realised that these were the homes of the dreaded Nusham, but that didn't seem to bother the other birds. They landed on the tables and tucked into the free meal.

Kos alighted on an ivy-covered ash tree and watched the goings-on from a safe distance. There was no food for him, but perhaps later a mouse would venture out for some of the spill-overs on the ground. He sat patiently, waiting, watching and listening. Different sounds could be heard here – the roar of a motorbike, a dog barking. Kos could see the Nusham sitting inside their houses. A small box flickered with pictures and made a lot of noise.

A little boy who was helping his father remove the snow from the path in a backyard noticed Kos perched high in the tree and called out excitedly: 'Daddy, look, an owl!'

'You don't get owls around here, son,' his Dad replied without raising his head to look. 'You have to go to the woods or the zoo for them.'

'But it's there!' replied the boy.

'Come on, son, it's time for tea, let's go in.'

The boy went reluctantly into the house holding his father's hand and keeping a fixed stare on Kos. A warm glow shone from the room. Kos blinked, the boy winked back, and the door closed. Things were quiet again.

A cat stalked the garden; then Kos noticed that all the birds were gone, probably back at their roost in the woods already. Night was closing in. He waited and waited, but no mouse appeared. Feeling cold, he ruffled his feathers to keep warm. He decided to leave, and he set off over the rooftops. White smoke wafted up from the chimneys, and little red sparks like stars danced through the smoke, then quickly disappeared. Flying high over the houses, Kos gave a shriek to the night air, but no one listened. He began to wonder whether he was flying in the right direction. He had followed the birds here, but they were now long gone and he realised that he hadn't paid much attention to the landmarks that could help him find his way back.

He continued to fly until he had left the Nusham houses behind, then on over broken-up fields with big yellow machines sitting in them. The silence of the night deepened. Flapping and gliding, he went over a countryside in the depths of winter. Icy winds stabbed at Kos's already chilled body. He knew he must force himself on to look for some familiar sign that would bring him home to the dark and warmth of the castle. This thought made him almost drowsy. He imagined himself pressed against his favourite part of the wall, asleep. His wings drooped, and he flew low over a winding, dark road, where the trees looked sinister as they hung over from each side of the verge and joined together in the middle in tangled growth.

Suddenly, through the aisles of darkness, came two piercing and blinding lights, heading straight for Kos. Dazzled and frightened, he just managed to veer to the right bank and avoid the car as it roared past at great speed. Kos stood still, but his heart pounded as he watched the car circle the winding roads and fade into the distance. A pool of silence descended.

Kos sat among the sheltering trees, shaking after the unnerving experience. He then became alert to something moving on the opposite bank; it was a cock chafer. It too had been disturbed by the car. It ventured from its hideout in the verge just far enough for Kos to swoop down and make an instant meal of it – not a lot for a hungry owl, but a welcome surprise.

Then away he flew again, across the sky which was now curtained with stars. The hedgerows cast silvery shadows on the bright snow. Crossing several fields,

Kos still could not recognise any familiar tree or post. Then he saw lights in the distance. Could it be the big house near his castle, he wondered? Well, there was only one way to find out, so he headed straight towards them.

Suddenly he heard a shriek that almost stopped him mid-flight. It was such a pleasing sound to him, knowing it could come from only one source, a barn owl like himself. A second shriek sounded long and loud; it was sweetness to his ears and there was something vaguely familiar in its tone. Without losing a moment, he flapped hard and moved towards that most welcome call.

He flew over a couple of fields, getting closer to the lights. They came from a house he had never seen before. Landing in a small field, he looked around cautiously. He could see lots of little wooden huts in a semi-circle, and inside were large birds sleeping on perches. He had never seen anything like these birds before. He noticed that they were all tied by one leg to their perches with a short cord. Some of the birds opened their eyes and stared fiercely at him. Across from the house were more wooden sheds with wooden bars over the windows. He heard another shriek, and it came from the sheds. Kos knew one of them must house a barn owl.

Landing on top of the first shed he peered in through the laths. Two large snowy owls stared back from their darkened cell.

'What do you want?' demanded the male snowy harshly, his yellow eyes staring hard through the laths.

Without replying, Kos moved away to the next compartment. Kos peered in – more owls, barred owls this time. They too snapped at Kos in a very unfriendly way.

'What's your business here?' they asked in unison.

Kos found it difficult to reply. Could the shriek have come from these barred owls, he wondered, or the large white ones beside them? He moved on again, leaving the owls bobbing from side to side.

'How did you get out?' asked a long-eared owl in the next shed.

'I didn't,' answered Kos. 'I was never in!'

'Aren't you the owl from next door?' asked the long-eared one.

'No,' replied Kos, 'I'm a barn owl!'

'I know you're a barn owl, silly. But aren't you young Driad?'

'Driad!' exclaimed Kos. 'But he's . . .'

Before Kos could finish what he was saying, Driad pressed his face against the thin strips of wood and gave out a loud shriek of joy. 'Kos!'

Kos could hardly believe his eyes and flew at the laths, gripping them tightly, hissing and snorting with excitement. 'Brother, I can't believe it's really you!'

They made such a raucous noise that the Nusham

came out from his house, beaming a torchlight in their direction.

'Quick,' said Driad. 'Hide!'

Kos flew away to a nearby beech.

'It's a wild barn owl come calling!' announced the Nusham to someone inside the house. 'I haven't seen one around these parts for some time.'

Swinging the torchlight in the direction of Kos, he paused for a moment, then went back inside. Kos watched the silhouette of the Nusham against the yellow light of the window. He waited for things to become quiet again.

After some time the lights in the house went out. Soon, the silence of the night returned and Kos flitted down to Driad.

'We'd better keep it quiet in case the Nusham comes out again. It's wonderful to see you, Kos!'

'You too. But how did you end up here?'

'Well, to cut a long story short, I was hit by a car while hunting near the verge of a road. When those car lights beamed so brightly into my eyes, they nearly blinded me!'

'The same thing happened to me,' said Kos. 'I nearly got flattened! It's the strangest creature I've ever seen!'

'It's not a creature,' said Driad, 'it's a machine that moves the Nusham about in a hurry. I felt my left wing being hit, then I must have passed out. I remember waking up hours later on the bank, unable to move.

I lay there all night and most of the morning, until a small Nusham came along, picked me up and brought me to this place.'

'That's terrible.'

'Oh, I suppose it could have been worse. The Nusham you saw a few moments ago fixed up my wing and put me here. We get fed every day and have a dry place to sleep. Lots of Nusham come and stare at us. You see, there are some very distinguished birds here – a golden eagle from Scotland, an imperial eagle from Spain, a bateleur and a tawny eagle from Africa. There are kites, buzzards, vultures, eagle owls, snowy owls, long-eared, barred and tawny owls. And, of course, kestrels, goshawks, peregrines, and sparrowhawks.'

'Wow!' said Kos. 'But you're all prisoners.'

'Don't use that word around here,' said Driad. 'It upsets everyone too much.'

'Sorry. But do you like it here?'

'No, I hate it, we all do. It's so boring it's killing us all slowly, if we were to admit it. I would love to soar in the starry sky again. It's the dream of escape that keeps us alive.'

'And you will escape,' said Kos, 'I promise!'

'No, it's impossible really, but we still have that dream. Sometimes when things get quiet around here, like when the Nusham are gone, we tell each other stories. The eagle has some wonderful tales to tell;

and as for the griffon vulture – we call him 'Griff' for short – he tells us about the amazing creatures that live near his home in Africa. Did you know there's an animal as tall as this shed, with ears bigger than both of us, and a nose as long as a branch?'

'That sounds like a tall story,' said Kos.

'It's true; it's called an elephant . . . But you look cold, you're shivering. Have you eaten?'

'Not much,' said Kos.

'Here, have this, go on, take it.' Driad passed a piece of raw meat to Kos, who gulped it down. 'We get food every day, more than enough. Sometimes we don't eat it all. Sitting around all day doesn't make you feel very hungry. Here, have some more. It has its compensations, being here!'

'Nothing can make up for the loss of sailing across the sky on a warm light wind,' Kos replied. 'I must get you out of here.'

'Impossible,' said Driad. 'The Nusham guard us very well, and there are dogs that patrol at night.'

'We must try,' insisted Kos.

'Would you like some more food?'

'No, I'm full – it's the first good meal I've had for ages. I remember Mother warning us that an owl could not survive any longer than five days without food . . .'

'How is she?' asked Driad.

Kos found it difficult to tell his brother of the tragic

death of Noctua. But when he finally did, Driad swelled up with grief and gave a loud shriek of despair that cut through the still night. The door of the house opened and there stood the Nusham, shining his torch, muttering to himself.

'It's that owl again . . .'

Kos flinched in fear and flew off to the cover of darkness. He spent the rest of the night huddled in the ivy on an elm tree, keenly missing the security of the castle; he felt anxious, but that gave way to the joy of meeting his brother again, even if he was imprisoned.

The night was long and cold. A tawny owl hooted once from his shadowy shelter. Kos sat, staring into the darkness, until tiredness finally overcame him and he slept.

CHAPTER VIII
Captured!

Kos woke to the early-morning clatter of noisy rooks who circled around the tall branches of the elms. He was perched over a small garden near the sheds of the falconry. A watery sun shone briefly in the sky. A robin picking at a morsel on a bird table was joined by a pair of chaffinches. They were quickly chased away by a mob of greedy starlings, voraciously eating the remaining food. Nearby, song thrushes and redwings were feeding on the red berries of the cotoneaster that bordered the garden. A cat stretched, then walked lazily along the roof. The tawny eagle gave a harsh, hungry call.

All the birds in the falconry were awake now; they began to preen and oil their feathers meticulously. The griffon vulture stretched his wings as if to take flight, flapped twice, then slowly folded them in again. The bateleur eagle showed his impressive crown as if in alarm, but then relaxed it.

Most of the birds seemed to be in good condition in spite of their predicament – all except the hen harrier, who was in a sorry state, for she had only one wing, the other having been shot clean off by a Nusham. This unbalanced her and occasionally she would accidentally step on her one wing and get herself into a tangled mess with the cord around her leg.

Sometimes a bird would bolt off his perch as if to fly away, but would only go a few feet and end up lying, wings spread out, on the snow. After a few moments, he would stagger to his feet and fly the length of the cord back to his perch.

Kos found this all very curious indeed. Although these birds appeared to be in peak condition, they all had a strange look – the look of confinement. And they were given to sudden outbursts of frustration, which they took out on each other verbally. The griffon was not unknown to take out his anger on himself, occasionally pecking savagely with his sharp beak at his wing until it bled. The old black vulture would have to talk to him in order to calm him down.

This morning the birds were busy pacing up and down and flapping, for they could sense that they were about to be fed. It was Monday and as a rule the Nusham did not feed them on Sunday. One day of fasting kept them lively, he believed, and they were all certainly lively this chilly Monday morning.

A kestrel, in his excitement, had managed somehow to tangle himself up so badly that he was left hanging upside down on his perch, wings extended, calling loudly in a piercing 'kee, kee, kee' sound. Kos was reminded of the time he had found his mother on the pole trap and flinched with the pain of the memory.

Finally, out came the Nusham, carrying several buckets of red meat, his black labrador trotting alongside him. He crunched his way through the snow and threw large pieces of meat at the golden eagle who immediately grabbed a bit in his strong yellow claws and, mantling it, proceeded to tear strips from it. The Nusham checked the jesses and rope around the eagle's feet to make sure they were safe, much to the annoyance of the bird. They looked secure and the Nusham moved on. The eagle then returned to eating.

Continuing the rounds, feeding and checking as he went along, the Nusham stopped to untangle the kestrel. Finally he fed the owls who were mostly snoozing, except for the eagle owl who put on an impressive threat display when he saw the dog. The dog barked loudly and the owl clicked and hissed.

'Quiet, you silly mutt!' said the Nusham in a loud voice to the dog and they both moved away. Soon he began to clear the snow from the pathways, and this job took him most of the morning.

Kos still had not moved from his perch in the branches. He was anxious to see Driad again, yet he knew he mustn't let the Nusham see him. He decided to wait until nightfall. After clearing most of the snow from the paths, the Nusham seemed to spend a lot of time placing something around the shed where Driad was kept.

The day seemed endless. Kos could not even sleep because he was discovered by some smaller birds. Great tits and blues, wrens, robins and a thrush all fluttered around, mobbing and scolding him. Why don't they mob and harass all those birds below in the sheds? Kos wondered. Perhaps they're used to them by now. Perhaps these little birds know that those big hawks and buzzards can't fly. Well, Kos was not going to budge until dusk. Finally, to his relief, the songsters got fed up and flew away.

At last the day faded and dusk descended. All seemed quiet. Raising his wings, Kos glided down over the sleeping kites, past the buzzard, then to the shed where Driad was. But as he was about to alight, he suddenly felt trapped, like a fly in a cobweb. He flapped his wings and clawed desperately with his feet, and his whole body became hopelessly tangled up. It was a mist-net which had been put there by the Nusham, and it was impossible to see it at night. Kos couldn't move. He shrieked loudly and pecked at the net.

Driad pressed his face through the wooden laths to see what was going on. All the birds sensed something; there was hissing and hooting; even the hawks were awake and kee-keeing. Kos was quivering with fear, and completely helpless.

'Got you, my beauty!' a voice called out. 'You'll make a suitable companion for the other one!' Little did the Nusham know that they were brothers.

In an instant he had removed Kos from the mist-net and was holding him by the legs. Opening a half-door into the shed, he flung Kos in.

'In you go, my beauty. You'll settle in fine after a couple of days!' Then he closed the half-door and left.

'Are you all right?' asked Driad anxiously.

'I think so,' said Kos. 'No feathers or bones broken . . .'

'Oh, it's all my fault,' said Driad. 'You wouldn't be here only for me.'

'It's my own fault for getting caught. Well, I wanted to see you and here we are. Let's make the best of it. We can make a plan to escape together,' said Kos reassuringly.

Looking away, Driad explained how lots of birds had tried to escape but none had ever succeeded.

'Only last week an eagle owl escaped while the Nusham was changing the jesses around his feet,' said

Driad. 'He flew off over the trees. We were all delighted and it gave us great hope that maybe it was really possible to be free. Four days later he was caught and brought back. He's now in a large cage on his own, away from the rest of us, and the guard dogs sit below him in their kennels.'

That evening when Nusham activity had ceased, the news about the new detainee quickly spread among the birds. Who was he, and why had he come here in the first place and allowed himself to be caught so easily? There were all kinds of theories about this: he had allowed himself to be caught

because he was on the verge of starvation, which sounded quite plausible; and the cara cara suggested, in very cautious tones, that 'he might even be a spy pretending to be a prisoner to find out more about us and our kind . . .' This idea made the kites and kestrels shudder in fear and it put the tawny eagle in a rage, until the griffon vulture dismissed it all as nonsense.

Finally Driad explained that Kos was his younger brother who had come seeking him, and told how he had been through many a bad experience recently, in particular the loss of their mother, and he emphasised the tragic way in which she had met her demise. This brought a flow of sorrow and compassion from the other birds. The snowy owl, in sympathetic tones, told of how he had tried to warn young Kos about the dangers of hanging around there. The barred owls chanted a sort of eulogy in memory of the mother barn owl, which was normally sung only for a close friend who had died or been killed:

> 'Fly now, radiant bird,
>   back to the bright skies of forever . . .'

Kos and Driad thanked them for their kind thoughts.

Next morning the Nusham came as usual with food. He peered in at Kos through the narrow wooden laths. 'How are you, my beauty?'

Kos immediately hunched his body, hung his wings low, extended his neck, snapped his bill and moved from side to side to try and look his most aggressive. He stared hard at the Nusham, putting on his best threat display. The Nusham just laughed with amusement and threw in some extra rations of meat.

Days passed, the snow finally disappeared, but it was still cold. Kos spent most of his days looking out through the wooden laths – day after tedious day. His imprisonment seemed worse when he watched a blackbird feeding on the lawn, or the sparrows busy on the garden wall.

Nusham would come to stare at them. Some young Nusham even poked sticks through the laths, and made the strangest hooting noises. Kos would occasionally shriek back. Driad would only blink at them with indifference.

For a time each day Kos would fly backwards and forwards in his cage and imagine he was circling the castle. He would try to get Driad to fly as well, but his brother felt it was a complete waste of time. Then Kos would look at the blue sky or the branches swinging in the wind; that gave him a lot of pleasure. He would never get used to this alien world of imprisonment. He noticed that the red kite had developed a permanent shiver and just huddled on his perch all day. Life should be lived like an adventure, thought Kos, not let slip away tediously like this. He watched one of his moulted feathers blow out into the air and drift over the trees on a light wind.

Driad told Kos many of the birds' stories and as there hadn't been a story-telling since his capture, Kos decided to tell about himself and Crag, the fox. He related his amusing tale about the pheasant and caused great merriment. All the birds were delighted with the story. Kos had won their trust.

Then the eagles told stories of faraway places and mountains that scraped the sky. Kos was intrigued. The snowy owl told of the cold and icy tundras, and how the animals there would change their brown summer fur into white for wintertime. The falcons told how they loved to soar across warm, welcoming skies; they said that they, as a species, were masters of the sky, and that their flying was the envy of other birds. This led to a heated argument from the hawks and eagles, who claimed they were just as graceful and proficient in the air.

When things got a little out of control the griffon vulture interrupted with strange and wonderful stories about his homeland. Even the other birds from Africa loved to hear the griffon relate his enchanting tales.

He spoke of the great river that started in the mountain and vanished many miles later into the desert; of the great herds that roamed the savannahs; of the water buffalo, the zebra, antelope, wildebeest, giraffe; the way the large cats hunted in the long grasses, ambushing the old or very young; and the crocodiles that lay with their mouths wide open by the river banks; the colourful birds that fed along the water's edge; snakes that could spit, and other larger snakes which coiled up in trees like long ropes, waiting to catch the monkeys jumping about the branches in order to squeeze the life out of them; the elephants that roamed about, finding water when the land was parched by digging with their long trunks.

He told how his own large family would circle the sky in search of food and how they could spot a dead animal a mile away; then they would all descend on the carcass and pick it clean to the bone under the warm sun. And in the evening they all slept together, high in an acacia tree, safe from jackals, lions and hyenas.

After the griffon had entertained them with such a splendid description of his homeland, Kos asked the kite to tell about where he lived or had visited. The kite looked surprised; in fact they all were, because since the kite had arrived he had never once told of any experiences, but had only listened. Finally, after a lot of encouragement, he began to tell of a land he had roamed where the elephants toiled for the Nusham, lifting tree trunks, carrying Nusham on their backs; and of cats called tigers, as big and strong as the lion, whose bodies were orange with black stripes; of beautiful Nusham palaces where the birds could nest in peace; of snowcapped mountains, the highest in the world. He also told of a strange

Nusham, covered with hair from head to toe, who wandered around the snow-covered mountains alone, and who was pursued in vain by the ordinary Nusham. All they ever found of the Snow-Nusham were his footprints.

'Well, that's about it . . .' he ended.

They were all very impressed and showed it by wing-flapping loudly. The owls just snapped their bills as their wings made no real sound. The kite threw a grateful glance to Kos. The buzzard was about to say something when suddenly the Nusham appeared carrying a box.

They all kept quiet and stared hard. He went inside one of the spare sheds, stayed a while and then came out, locked it and went away. The birds knew it must be a new arrival, for the Nusham always used that box for carrying smaller kestrels or owls. Filled with curiosity, they could hear the sound of wings flapping against the lathed window.

'He'll injure himself,' said Kos, as he listened to the unfortunate bird knocking himself off the wood.

After a time a male sparrowhawk appeared at the window, trembling with fear and shock, his breath rasping. The other birds became watchful and tense.

Finally the golden eagle asked in gentle tones what the matter was, for they knew the hawk was unusually stressed, as he had made his forehead bleed badly. With a little more coaxing he finally told them how the Nusham had invaded the oak woods where he and his ancestors had lived for generations, and how in one day they had coldly and cruelly torn down the great woods – tree after tree sent crashing to the gound by a chain-saw.

'Then the saplings and bushes were torn up by big yellow machines, making ugly scars through the undergrowth where the bluebells, snowdrops and primroses grew, scooping everything up in a big pile.

'The branches were all cut off the big trees and the long logs were stacked on top of a truck and taken away. Then the diggers moved in to grub up the roots, the broken saplings and the homes of all the creatures. Everything was churned up; all day and night, clanking and grinding, banging and shouting, until the whole place had been tortured. The scars ran deep. The woods looked a terrible mess.

'A lot of small creatures perished – squirrels, hedgehogs, pinemartens, small birds. Some flew to safety, but most hid in the cut piles and perished in the great fire that followed . . .

'I escaped when it first began but later flew back

over the ravaged woods, where I could hear the muffled cries of maimed and dying creatures. I then flew for miles and miles until my body ached with tiredness, and I finally took shelter in an old barn.

'I was roused from half-sleep to see a Nusham coming slowly towards me holding a large coat in his two hands. His voice sounded friendly. Then he threw the coat over me, and I was put in a box. I was left in darkness for some time, but I could hear lots of sounds. And I ended up here.'

There was a stunned silence as the sparrowhawk ended his horror story. Despair gave way to towering rage. The buzzard asked why the Nusham hated the woods so much.

'It's not so much that they hate the woods; it's that they just don't care. They probably want to build more Nusham houses. I've seen it happen in so many places,' said the eagle owl gravely.

Then the sparrowhawk turned away and hid in the dark shadows of the hut. The birds fell silent. The hawk's words racked them all with pain and anger, and continued to pull at their minds all through the night as they relived the nightmarish image.

* * *

The grey skies of morning brought little relief, for when the Nusham came around to feed the hawk he found him lying in a pathetic, dead heap in a corner of the hut, a bluebottle wandering over the corpse. As the Nusham came out carrying the limp body, he too looked grieved at the passing of the sparrowhawk. When he left, the barred owls chanted their eulogy:

'Fly now, radiant bird,
back to the bright skies of forever . . .'

The griffon reared up his head and, with outstretched wings, began to make a snake-like movement with his neck, pecking in frustration at the grey rope that imprisoned him.

'I've had it!' he announced sharply. 'I'm getting out!'

He would escape the next day, he said, and that was a promise. He spent that whole day pecking at the rope. He pecked fiercely until he began to make small slits in it. He yearned for the warm sun of Africa, the skies where he could soar on long, stretched wings for hours at a time – and the thought of this kept him going. Freedom was what he wanted and freedom was what he was going to get. He worked on into the last hours of light.

The birds awaited the morning with great expectations. The first rays of the early-morning sun saw the griffon still pecking at the long rope that tied him to the block. Finally it was done. Shouting his farewells to all the inmates, he raised his large wings anxiously, knowing it was now or never.

'I'm going home!' he shouted, flexing his wings. He flapped with all his might. The great wings, long unused to flight, took a while to get airborne, but soon, with a surge of energy, the large griffon vulture rose up into the sky, the rope still hanging from one foot.

The birds watched in excitement as Griff courageously took flight. He made a huge, black shadow against the sky as he veered over the trees, leaving his prison behind.

'I'm going to the land beyond the great ocean!' he shouted as he circled higher and higher.

The birds flapped their wings with joy. The guard dogs barked furiously and the Nusham rushed out only to witness the griffon disappear over the far beech trees and out of sight.

A mysterious tranquillity pervaded the falconry. The birds spoke in whispers, too excited even to eat.

'He had great courage to take off like that after so long in this prison,' Driad said to Kos.

'We'll do it too,' said Kos. 'You wait and see; if only we could find an opening we'd be off too!'

The Nusham was furious at losing one of his prize birds. He had had it for ten years and it had been the only one of its kind in the country. Adults and children had travelled for miles to see it.

He informed the local police and newspapers. The

Ornithology Club was also on the lookout. There was nothing else to do now but wait. A bird like that would surely be noticed and soon he would have it back again, he hoped. Tomorrow might bring some good news.

Soon the landscape was wrapped in darkness. A soft hoot from the long-eared owl floated through the still night.

Next morning the birds were still talking about Griff. They wondered if he had reached Africa yet. The swallows and other birds travelled to Africa and back each year. If they could do it, it should be easy for a large bird like Griff. He could probably make the journey in half the time, thought the cara cara.

'It will take about two cycles of the moon,' said the buzzard.

'It's a very long way and the weather is very unpredictable,' added the kestrel.

The birds spent most of the day debating the journey: the distance Africa was from the falconry; where he would stop to eat; would he remember the way there; had he met any other bird of his kind for company?

Then the Nusham appeared through the gates of the falconry, looking very distressed and carrying a large black bag. He walked past the black vultures, stopped at the griffon's perching block, pulled up the wooden sign written clearly in black – 'Griffon Vulture' – and went into the house. What could this mean, the birds wondered. They must find out, but how? The golden eagle had an idea – they could ask the grey heron who lived and roosted in the cedar nearby.

It was a long wait until the heron finally appeared in the evening sky. She didn't have to be called, for she landed in the circular grass patch from where one could get a clear view of most of the birds, and then she told them: 'I know you're wondering about your friend, the vulture called Griff. Well, I'm sorry to be the one to tell you, but he's dead, found drowned in the canal less than a mile from here.'

There was a deep silence as the heron related the terrible news.

'It seems he landed on one of the trees that overhang the water. He had a long rope tied to his leg and somehow it got tangled around one of the branches. He must have panicked and fallen from the bough into the dark water; his wings got waterlogged and, sadly, he drowned . . .'

The birds flinched with pain at every word. It grieved them that their old friend should come to his end in such a terrible way. Their hopes were dashed by Griff's death. The cold winds of despair blew through the falconry. The heron took off silently, the birds were too sad even to thank her.

'He didn't get a mile away,' said the cara cara, 'not even a mile.'

Once again they all chanted in unison their lament for a special bird:

> 'Fly now, radiant bird,
> back to the bright skies of forever . . .'

A light rain began to fall, soon becoming heavier, lashing down on the birds as they sat huddled quietly on their blocks. Kos's moist black eyes looked out from the shadows, and he vowed that soon he would be free.

CHAPTER IX

The Dark Kingdom

Night brought a blanket of dense fog over the land; it drifted slowly over the fields, settling in places around the woods and on the quiet river. The sky was dark, the moon had not yet risen. A large, black shape moved restlessly over the ground, sniffing and scurrying, alert to any sign of danger. It was Fericul.

He slipped under some barbed wire and was followed by Hack, Spike and Thrasher. They were in a large field now, far away from the security of the city dump.

Two horses stood like statues in the middle of the field, oblivious to the rats whose rippling bodies ran along the fringes of the river. The cry of a curlew briefly disturbed the stillness of the night. Hack wondered how much further they would have to go, for it seemed they had been travelling all night, yet he dared not ask for he was more than aware of the moods of Fericul at this stage.

Fericul stopped up ahead, the others some distance behind him. It was hard going keeping up with the Emperor when he was on the move. His energy seemed endless and, despite his heavy frame, he moved very swiftly over this difficult terrain.

Suddenly he stopped. He had spotted a lapwing's nest. The bird called in alarm, but her soft 'pee-weet' call and swooping did not deter Fericul from gorging on the eggs he found there. The lapwing continued to circle in distress, and even resorted to feigning a broken wing and swerving about in a tizzy.

'Up here,' Fericul called, and the others advanced slowly.

'Hmmm, a pleasant snack!' Fericul said, after he had finished three of the four eggs. Egg yolk spilled from the sides of his mouth. 'There is one left for you,' he added.

Hack, Thrasher and Spike fought over the last egg, finally spilling its contents across the nest. They lapped up the warm liquid, then moved on, leaving the lapwing darting fearfully about and surveying the destruction of her nest by the raiding party. Her plaintive cry could be heard for a long time afterwards.

Gradually a slender silver crescent moon brightened the ebony night sky. Fericul moved feverishly on over crumbling moss-covered walls.

'We're very near!' he shouted in tones of great excitement as they passed several denuded trees whose twisted forms stood like sentinels guarding ancient secrets. Pausing for a moment, he pointed across to some large, carved stones, behind which was a circular white stone building, which seemed to rise out of the hillock. Above it long grasses grew.

'We're here!' announced Fericul. 'Well, what do you think?'

The other rats shivered in doubtful approval as they sat in the grave-like stillness.

Without waiting for their response, Fericul moved speedily towards the sacred site. The quest was over for the night prowlers. They had finally arrived at RATLAND.

A tingle of fear shook the three follower rats as they watched the Emperor enter the shadowy passage. Cautiously picking their way over the carved entrance stones, they disappeared after him into the blackness. It took some time for their eyes to grow accustomed to the dark.

Looking behind, they could see the doorway framing the luminous night. The fog had vanished as quickly as it had appeared. Moving on through the stone-carved tunnel, they could see Fericul skulking

about in the meagre light ahead of them. They went after him into a large circular chamber with strange Nusham markings on the walls.

Cobwebs wove a heavily patterned curtain from the ceiling to the ground. With a wave of his paw, Fericul cut through the intricate pattern. A spider appeared momentarily, quickly recoiled and fled to a hole in the wall.

Fericul picked up something off the ground, then suddenly swung round and flung a Nusham skull at the others. They ducked down just in time, only to witness it smashing off the stone wall and breaking like an eggshell. He could see they were startled and this brought roars of laughter from him, which echoed through the many tunnels.

'Let's move!' he said in gruff tones.

The next tunnel, leading down to lower regions, seemed even more weird to the rats. For, instead of stones, the walls were built with skulls of rodents, thousands of them piled on top of each other, battered and sunken forms that stared through empty sockets. Then they came to a honey-combed chamber with a large stone, like a monolith, in the centre. This stone was deeply cut with a carving of a rodent, sitting in an upright position. Fericul pulled a shiny object from underneath. He pressed on this with all his might and it clicked several times until finally a single flame appeared. He touched the flame to a small bundle of dry grass which instantly ignited into a warm, blazing fire. The other three were truly amazed.

'See, my comrades, we have the gift of fire. This was a gift from Rattus to me before he turned traitor. It was taken from the Nusham. So now we have found our ancient home, and the magic fire lighter. But there are many more wondrous things to come. Soon we will live here again in the Kingdom of the Great Rat Lords, now my kingdom!'

And the four rats sat huddled before the great fire that held back the darkness, while cheerless shadows were cast by the many skulls that made up the walls.

CHAPTER X

The Great Escape

Early one morning a large flock of rooks descended to the ground in the falconry. They came mainly to jeer and tease the hawks and to raid the many bins that usually held morsels of food discarded by the Nusham.

The rooks strode around to all the birds huddled on their concrete blocks. One cheeky fellow pulled at the tail feathers of the sleepy black vulture. He flapped his big wings in annoyance, but this only amused the rooks. Kos watched through the laths while the other owls, including Driad, were doing what comes naturally to them in daytime – sleeping.

Suddenly, Kos noticed his friend, Shimmer, alight on the cut lawn and begin to peck among the daisies.

Kos called out: 'Shimmer! Shimmer!'

The rook looked around, surprised that any of the birds here should know him. He flew towards the shed and peered in.

'It's you!' he said in surprise. 'How did you manage to get yourself locked up here?'

'It's a strange story,' Kos replied. 'You see, this owl beside me here is my brother, Driad. I came to meet him and got caught myself.'

'What are you going to do?' Shimmer asked.

'We must escape,' said Kos.

'How can I help?' asked the rook.

'Well, we need someone to cut through the leather lock on the door.'

'My beak is strong, but it wouldn't manage to pierce through that leather. It would take hours, maybe days. I'm sorry.'

'Oh, I didn't mean you to do it, but could you ask the red fox that lives near the farm?'

'Old Crag, you mean?' said Shimmer. 'Well, I don't know. I'm wary of all foxes and old Crag is no exception. I've seen him catch a magpie that was annoying him, by leaping into the air. He's not to be trusted.'

'Oh, please,' said Kos, 'he's the only one I know who could manage it.'

'Okay, I'll try. I hate to see my young friend locked up. I'm off now and I'll look for him today. He could even be here by tonight. Good luck.'

'Thank you, thank you very much . . .' shouted Kos, as he watched Shimmer's black form move across the morning sky followed by the rest of the rooks.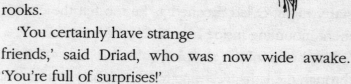

'You certainly have strange friends,' said Driad, who was now wide awake. 'You're full of surprises!'

'He'll come, I know it!' said Kos.

There was great excitement in the falconry, for word got around quickly about the planned escape. It was just as well the Nusham did not understand bird language, for the cara cara was blurting it out to everything that moved. There was a high level of excitement all day.

The golden eagle called to Kos. He had the warmth of age in his voice. He made a moving little speech: 'This might be the greatest challenge of your life, white owl. If you succeed, you will do it for all of us. You are vibrant with life, we believe in you, we know you can do it!

'Our wings have grown tired, our eyes weak; it's up to you to fly free in the great skies for us all, but especially for Griff. You have a special place in all our hearts. It is you who will reach the unreachable sky;

it will be your domain! It was mine once; we all shared it, so many memories away. Good luck, my friend. You will be flying for us all . . .'

The eagle's speech made it even more important for Kos to escape. He circled the shed, flexing his wings, hoping that Crag would not fail him. He imagined the wild winds catching his wings on a clear starry night. Driad preened as he too felt the excitement mounting inside him, but he did not show it.

The bustle of the morning subsided. Kos watched through the laths, yearning for the night, his stomach fluttering with nerves. The day seemed endless; hour followed tedious hour. They sat, watching and waiting, as the day drifted slowly by.

The sun was beaming its last light before sinking behind the trees when a whistling noise of wings was heard as the mallard ducks took their evening flight before roosting on the lake. Finally darkness hugged the falconry.

Kos heard his name being called in a hushed voice. Pressing his face hard against the laths, he saw Crag's amber eyes staring up at him.

'Well, there you are, my dear little owl. I called many times to the castle looking for you. Glad to see you're okay.'

'Oh, yes, it's good to see you,' gasped Kos in wild excitement.

'Well, let's see if my old teeth can bite through this!'

All the birds listened as Crag bit and chewed through the thick leather. He could sense many inquisitive eyes staring at him from the darkness. Crag growled, and twisted his jaws around the leather. He was managing to bite through it! Kos watched Crag strain, pull and twist his body with all his might to break the leathery lock. Suddenly, to his horror, he saw one of the rottweilers sneaking up through the nettles towards Crag, his large jaws dripping with saliva. Crag seemed oblivious to the danger, he was concentrating so hard.

'Watch out!' Kos shrieked with all his might. 'Behind you!' Crag leaped into the air as the dog lunged for him, his savage, snapping jaws biting at fresh air as Crag bolted through the falconry to the nearby fields.

A second dog, this time the black labrador, joined the rottweiler and they took off in hot pursuit of the fox. Kos could see that the door was marginally ajar.

'Come on, Driad, let's go. This is our chance!' Driad seemed locked in fear. 'Driad, it's now or never!'

They could hear the heavy steps of the Nusham on the gravel path, torch flashing wildly, scanning through the darkness.

Kos prised his body through the gap in the door, tearing some feathers from his shoulders.

'I'm out. Come on, Driad, you can do it!'

Driad shivered and rocked his body. He could hear Kos calling, and the quickening footsteps of the

Nusham who now realised what was happening.

'Now!' shouted Kos, circling outside.

Driad wavered, then finally found his wings and flew at the opening. He squeezed and pushed. The Nusham was almost upon him, his hands outstretched to close the door. Driad cleared the door just as it slammed behind him.

'Blast!' shouted the Nusham, as Driad and Kos took flight.

Driad was a little unsure of himself, the night sky looked so big.

But Kos was in his element, wheeling and circling overhead!

'FREE!' shrieked Kos. 'FREE . . .!' His words rang around the falconry. All the birds were awake, flapping their wings, 'kee-keeing' and bill-snapping.

The Nusham swore and threw his hat to the ground in annoyance. Then the two owls circled the huts and shouted farewell to their friends. They flew away over the swaying trees, out on the night winds, to freedom.

There was great joy in their flight. They played games – one flew above the other, trying to make one shadow on the ground. They flew side by side, almost touching. They felt the wind rise up under their wings. Driad had not tasted freedom for a long time, and he was ecstatic.

Kos noticed the old folly where he had perched once or twice, and knew they were heading in the

right direction for home. As they passed near the folly they saw Crag below, sitting on a large stone. They swooped down, shrieking loudly to him.

Crag was panting hard. 'We did it,' he said, trying to control his panting. 'We outwitted the Nusham!'

'What happened to the dogs?' Driad asked cautiously.

'Oh, I out-foxed them!' He grinned. 'I left a heavy scent in the ditch. They're probably still scratching around there. But I'm exhausted.'

'That's enough excitement for one evening,' Driad said. 'We'd all better get home to sleep.' They both thanked Crag, said they hoped to see him soon, and then, on hushed wings, headed for the castle. Crag loped off through the woods to his den.

Kos and Driad flew together over the dark, ancient walls of the castle. They slipped through the window into the secret passage that was their home and roost. Settling inside, they pressed themselves against the wall and ruffled their feathers. They were safe and secure inside these enduring walls which they held so dear. Finally, drowsiness overtook them, their facial discs folded in slowly and they slept soundly in the safety of their own home.

CHAPTER XI

The Storm before the Calm

One evening Driad and Kos awoke to the sound of crashing thunder. Jagged streaks of lightning lit up the thunderous skies and sheets of rain pelted down. Kos watched as it cascaded down the castle walls. The torrential rain had washed over the countryside, swelling the river, which burst its banks and spilled out, flooding the nearby fields and meadows.

'We won't be able to do much flying in this weather,' said Driad, sitting alongside Kos. 'Our feathers would get waterlogged and we wouldn't be able to see either.'

Kos gave a knowing nod, letting Driad know he had no intention of venturing out, even though he was feeling peckish. Then, to his surprise, he spotted two dead rats under an overhanging stone of the castle.

'Look!' he said excitedly. 'Food!'

They both leaped outside, snatched the food and hurried back again. Even in those few moments they got quite wet. The rats had been killed recently, a couple of hours ago at most, Kos thought.

'That's strange. But it has happened before, you know; I've found food lying around. I wonder was it left specially for us?'

'But by whom?' inquired Driad, feeling very grateful for the food. 'Maybe your crow friend, Shimmer? It would be some job for a rook to catch two fat rats!'

Kos was puzzled. It couldn't have been Crag, for he would not have been able to climb to that point of the castle.

The owls rested while the storm passed, its fury finally spent. The driving curtains of rain were gone. A light sprinkling drizzle followed, falling gently on the countryside. It, too, stopped before the first star appeared in the sky. Tranquillity descended and the air was filled with a delightful fragrance.

'We'll get out after all,' said Kos, peering from the darkness at the quiet skies.

'You go ahead; I'll follow later,' said Driad.

'I think I'll check on my foxy friend,' said Kos, and out he flew on to the castle wall. He hissed, ruffled his feathers, preened a little. Finally, raising his wings, he was off through the still air, over the trees and on towards the lake.

Dabbling ducks could be seen on the water, unaware of the silent observer overhead. On he flew, past a small copse of birch, oak and rowan, over some blackthorn and past the elder, to where Crag lived. He alighted on some brambles with a loud hiss to let Crag know of his presence.

The fox replied with a yelp of gladness as he emerged from his earth.

'What a storm!' said Kos.

'Oh, when you've lived through as many storms as I have, you hardly notice them,' said Crag. 'Still, it was impressive.'

'They're exciting to watch,' remarked Kos.

'Not as exciting as catching a tasty young hare!' said Crag – and with that he bolted suddenly from the earth and tore after a hare which was bounding along the edge of a field. The hare stopped, sat bolt upright, then quickened its pace as it spotted Crag hot on its heels. They raced around the ploughed field, a few clever twists and turns by the hare sending Crag running off in several wrong directions until finally the hare leapt through a fence and was gone into a distant field.

Crag wandered back slowly, panting heavily.

'You nearly had him!' said Kos.

'No,' said Crag, 'Droopy Ears is far too fast for an old fox like me. I just do it for the fun!'

'Wait there,' said Kos. 'I'll try to catch you something,

but it won't be a hare, that's for certain!'

'There's no need, really. Asrai will be back soon with some food. You remember her?'

Kos nodded.

'You know, Asrai is named after the small fairies of the ancient woods,' said Crag proudly. 'The legends say that if you try to catch them they turn into water. And my Asrai is well named. She loves swimming; she'll even go into a lake after a moorhen or duck.'

'How did you meet?' asked Kos.

'Well, by chance really. It was on a clear winter's night. She was wandering sadly across a field. You see, her mate had been killed by a hedge-trap – a vile Nusham trap. They have devised many kinds of traps for wild folk.'

Kos was silent, listening intently.

'I invited her to share a wood-pigeon I had found; she declined but I met her again the next evening and we became mates. She's an excellent hunter and provides most of the food. I'm fed on the finest rabbits when we're together.'

Suddenly Bawson the badger came towards them, looking very anxious. Kos immediately went into a threat display.

'It's okay,' said Crag calmly. 'It's my good friend, Bawson!'

The badger reported a big increase in the number of black rats near the woods of the great house.

'I was foraging on the outskirts, grubbing for worms, when I saw them, like an army, at least fifty . . . no, more, a hundred, all moving together across the dirt track.'

'What could be going on?' wondered Crag.

'I went over to get a closer look,' continued Bawson, 'when the leader sprang at me and gave me a bad gash below the eye. He was nearly as big as a cat, honest! And vicious. I've never experienced anything like it. I found it hard to shake him off.

'I'm no coward, as you know, but I ran in fear of my life. The other rats hissed, squealed and jeered at me as I got myself away from there.'

Bawson felt a little ashamed for running away – he who once took on two terrier dogs that were trying to bait him. The strongest animal in the area, chased away by a few rats! But Crag consoled him, reminding him of his past acts of bravery, and that brightened him up somewhat.

Then Crag introduced Kos to Bawson.

'He's from the Donadea Castle clan.'

'Oh, very good,' said Bawson. 'I know your family. Be careful when you're out hunting. There's something strange going on. I can feel it in my bones. Good-bye for now,' said Bawson and off he went as suddenly as he had come, moving his stout frame soundlessly through the undergrowth.

'I'm fond of old Bawson,' said Crag. 'He's a bit

moody at times, but he's a good friend. He gets weird dreams sometimes, but they're usually a warning of some great event about to take place. He told me once I would meet a vixen with a black belly. I laughed, but at the next full moon I met Asrai who comes from a black-bellied race, unusual in these parts.'

'That's amazing,' said Kos.

'You'd better head off now if you're to get in any hunting,' advised Crag.

'Yes,' replied Kos, 'And I'm to meet Driad. Good-bye for now.'

Then off he went, silently beating his way over some horses asleep in a field, then flying low, dipping and floating in the gloom. He wondered where all the rats were that Bawson spoke of. He travelled over several fields and gave a loud shriek that was lost on the night air. A snipe passing in twisted flight was headed for his home in the peaty black bog. There was no sign of Driad. Maybe he was back at the castle already?

The moon appeared from behind the clouds as Kos flew deeper into the night. He would slow up, hover a bit, then move on. Nothing was abroad tonight except himself. He would flap for a while, then slip into a glide again to probe the ground below.

Then he noticed the most amazing thing – it was a small moon in a box beside a field! What a wonderful sight, he thought, I must get a closer look. Landing alongside a feeding trough, he peered in, not knowing that many a poor owl had met a watery death in such a place as this.

Kos adjusted his position until he could see right in, and this time not only did he see the moon, but a lovely white owl staring back at him. How amazing!

He leaned forward to touch it and the other owl did exactly the same. Kos hissed in greeting. He jumped towards the stranger, but to his horror, he was suddenly caught in water. He flapped and twisted but this only made things worse, for his body was now becoming waterlogged. Shuddering in terror, he could see the blurred shape of the moon shining as he slipped down into the deep, treacherous water whose invisible clutch would bring him to a watery death.

Then alert eyes darted towards him. Splashing through the water came animal jaws. Kos felt their grip, and then darkness!

Crag lay drowsing on a moss-covered rock, his brush covering his face. Then, through the silvery night came Asrai. Crag raised his head and focused his sleepy eyes. To his horror he could see she was carrying a white owl in her jaws.

'Oh, no!' he exclaimed. 'You haven't killed my little friend, Kos?'

CHAPTER XII

Spring in the Air

Early the following morning, Asrai picked her way through a bank of pale yellow primroses, stopping briefly to sniff the ferns, which were alive with so many scents. Her nose twitched and she sneezed from the dust of the young ferns. Through the stillness of the dewy green morning she could see Crag and Kos, who was still looking bedraggled from his soaking the previous night, sitting among the wood anemones at the base of the oak and chatting away. Asrai was glad to see Crag contented. He loved to talk, and the stories would all be new to the owl, stories which she had heard so many times before, and which always became more embellished in the retelling.

Swishing her tail in greeting, Asrai joined them. Crag nudged her body as she circled around them, her brush spreading across his face. Nearby, a black-bird scolded from a thicket.

Then she dropped three fieldmice from her mouth. 'Eat up! You too, Kos.'

'She looks after me like a mother,' said Crag, 'and I'm nearly twice her age!'

'That's why!' Asrai replied, as she licked his ears and face fondly.

They bolted down the mice. Above them a tree-creeper roamed the bark of the oak searching for insects. Kos preened his damp feathers and held out his wings to let the early-morning sun dry them. Crag was so pleased that his little friend had survived.

'Thank you, Asrai, for saving me last night,' said Kos.

'I was glad to be able to do it. Crag and Bawson think you're destined for great things, and so do I.' Kos looked puzzled. 'And there are not many owls who spend the night in a fox's den,' she said.

'And live to tell the tale,' added Crag. 'He's got more lives than a cat, this one has!'

They all laughed loudly, then Asrai took herself off into the undergrowth, silent as a shadow. Crag watched her disappear from view.

'Soon she'll have young ones,' Crag said. 'It'll be our second litter together.'

'That's wonderful!' said Kos.

'It is,' said Crag. 'She's gone now to her secret earth

in the woods where the deep shadows fall. Soon, in the soft bed of bracken, they'll arrive. It's a very exciting time indeed. Well, I'd better rest my old bones.'

Kos blinked in the sunlight. Maybe he should fly back to the castle and tell Driad that he was okay?

'I'd better be away, Crag. See you soon and thanks again.'

Crag lifted his drowsy head. 'Goodbye! Be careful flying back. Remember you don't have the cover of darkness and you'll probably be mobbed by those pesky magpies before you reach the castle.'

'I'll be careful, don't worry,' said Kos, and off he went, wafting his way over the meadow, thinking of the previous night, and of falling into the water, a memory so scary that he knew he would never forget it as long as he lived. He looked down with pleasure on the fields far below. This was something Crag would never experience, Kos realised, unless he sat high on a hill, but that was not the same as flying over the trees and fields.

It must be very strange only ever managing to view things at ground level, he mused. This thought made him glad to be a bird. The warm sun felt good on his back; the gentle flow of wind over his feathers soon dried him. He was back to his own self again, gliding slowly and gently, with a few wing strokes, over the fields.

From an alder tree a chiff-chaff called. A speckled wood-butterfly danced in the air below. Rabbits nibbled at the edge of a field – the grasses were more yellow where the rabbits had been eating. A kestrel shook the wind from her wings and dropped to the ground.

Kos had never experienced spring before. He had thought that winter would continue forever. What a pleasant surprise it was to see leaves on trees that had been bare for so long. And the singing of the songsters, their liquid melodies, were wonderful sounds to his ears – if only he could sing like that!

Alighting on a mossy tree stump, he checked through his feathers. A robin on a nearby branch opened its delicate beak and poured forth its spring song. The sticky buds on the horse-chestnut attracted buzzing insects with a promise of plenty. The wood-floor was soft and spongy, fragile shoots springing up everywhere. All the birds were in their summer plumage, some in courtship – like the great-crested grebes who danced their own ritual on the lake. Sparrowhawks were circling in the sky above each other, their display equally graceful to watch. Frogs were already mating and spawning. The whole countryside seemed to be a hive of activity.

Kos watched the swallows skimming over the fields. It made him think of the birds in the falconry talking about the little fork-tails from Africa who came to visit these parts. He felt sad when he thought of poor Griff the vulture, who had so wanted to get home to Africa and sit on his favourite acacia tree.

Passing over the lake he observed Sheila, the heron, stalking the water, watching for the slightest ripple of movement. Further on a moorhen went into deep cover in the reeds. From a willow tree a willow warbler announced his arrival.

Sailing buoyantly over the trees, Kos was spotted by a couple of magpies, for he was near their nest. They flew at him, mobbing him mercilessly. One pecked him on the back, and the beak pierced through Kos's skin, causing a sharp pain. Luckily, he was near the castle. He sped over the wall and inside to the safety of his roost. The magpies continued scolding, in harsh, rattling tones from outside the castle wall. Kos shrieked back.

Driad opened his black eyes. 'I'm glad you're all right. I was worried sick. I searched everywhere for you!'

'Well, I did get into a bit of trouble, but the foxes came to my rescue. I spent the night in their den.'

'What!' Driad gasped. He couldn't believe what he was hearing.

'They seem to think I'm destined for something!'

'Kos, remember you're an *owl*,' said Driad in his big-brother tone. 'You should act like one – hunting, resting, preening and eventually raising a family. That's an owl's life.'

Kos agreed, but he felt that there could be more to life as well. Then he remembered something the fox had told him. 'You know when a tree has been cut, and the circles on the stump can be seen clearly?'

'Yes,' said Driad indifferently.

'Well,' said Kos, 'Crag says that those rings are for each summer the tree has known. The wide gaps between them show a good growth, good wet years, and the thin, close rings show the very dry summers. Isn't that amazing?'

'Yes,' said Driad, 'now let's sleep.'

Kos looked out through the narrow window. He could see the moon faintly in the blue sky. 'I wonder why the moon stays out after the night is gone, lingering on into the morning? Do you know, Driad?'

'Go to sleep, Kos . . .' yawned Driad.

*   *   *

Dusk seeped like silt across the trees, merging with the wood's grey shadows. The trees loomed darkly against the sky. Kos awoke, hissed and moved from the shadows to the wall.

Below, a deer was eating the tender young shoots and seedlings at the edge of the wood. Woodcocks were roding as they flew over the conifers, and a distant hoot came from within the woods.

Kos stretched, hissed, and meticulously checked his feathers, spreading oil from his gland on to them. Pipistrelle bats flitted about in search of moths. Two more woodcocks passed over the woods.

Kos gave one loud shriek and dropped from the castle wall. His beating wings made no sound as he passed over a hedgehog ambling along the dirt track. He stopped briefly in mid-flight to catch a moth, then on again, silently prowling the night in search of food.

A second hoot floated softly through the air. Deciding to investigate, Kos moved soundlessly through the dark. He circled in and out of the trees but could see nothing. Then, alighting on a beech stump at the edge of the woods he watched the meadow, listening for the rustle of mice, or the squeak of shrews.

The moon was directly behind Kos, and he could see the long shadow his own body cast across the field in front of him. When he opened his wings, his shadow seemed as big as the vulture in the falconry. Closing one wing, then the other, he flapped furiously, then he spread out his wings, trying to make different shapes by turning his body sideways, or crouching low.

If Driad could only see me now, he thought. Then he wondered why Driad had gone out so early without even waking him. Where does Driad go hunting? Driad seemed edgy lately.

Casting such thoughts aside, Kos returned to making strange shadowy shapes. Tucking his head under one wing, and opening the other, he twisted his head to see what kind of un-owlish shadow he had made this time. Then, standing bolt upright, he stretched out his wings as wide as they could go, but when he looked again he saw *two* shadows with outstretched wings.

What was this? He folded his wings and looked again. There was another shadow alongside his, its

wings still outstretched. This could mean only one thing. Swivelling his head anxiously, he saw behind him the dark shape of an owl against the moon.

'Don't be alarmed,' said a gentle voice. 'My name is Barkwood. I live in these parts. I knew your family.'

Kos relaxed as the long-eared owl landed beside him.

'You seemed to be having fun!' said the stranger.

'Oh, just fooling around. My name is Kos.'

'I know, and your brother is Driad. You live in Donadea Castle. You were missing for some time. I thought you had deserted the place or something.'

'Oh, no,' said Kos. 'I was caught, and taken prisoner in a falconry.'

'That's terrible,' said Barkwood. 'I would hate that. You've been through a lot for a fellow as young as you.'

'You knew my family well?' Kos asked.

'Oh, yes. Your parents had no offspring for years, and then two broods came along in the same year. Hoolet and Noctua were very special owls. I remember the dreadful night she was killed.'

'Were you there?' asked Kos.

'Yes. I heard her screams, I'll never forget them. By the time I got to her, old Crag and his young vixen were there. I knew there was nothing I could do then, so I just watched from a nearby tree.'

'Was it you who left food at the castle for me?' asked Kos.

Barkwood nodded.

'Thank you . . .'

'Well, you remind me of your father. He was a great friend of mine,' said Barkwood.

'What happened to him?'

'It was tragic,' said Barkwood sadly.

Kos's heart sank. 'Please tell me,' he coaxed.

'It was autumn and there was a harvest moon. I was hunting near the ditches not far from the woods. Your father passed by at the same time each evening, taking the same route. He would see me and give his big shriek, always taking me by surprise.

'That night was no exception. I flew to a gate post

and he swooped over to join me. I knew he had been out earlier than I, since he had a second brood to feed. I would tease him about clearing all the mice out of the fields.

'He circled the woods that morning, covering many of the fields, then came back. "Nothing moving," he said, disappointed.

'I told him there were lots of bats about. "More trouble than they're worth," said Hoolet. "You must have cleared all the rodents from the fields with your hooting! I'll try those distant fields where mice and rats often go at this time of year."

'"The Nusham were busy over there all day," I told him.

'"Good," said Hoolet. "Maybe they disturbed the rat population. Like to join me?"

'"No thanks," I said. "I've had a mouse, a bat and two beetles already. I don't have a hungry brood to feed, like you."

'He flew off then. I saw him go back and forth to the castle several times during the night; he seemed to have plenty of success. After the owlets were full, then and only then would he himself eat.

'It was about midnight, and there was a light mist over the fields when he arrived over to me after searching for some supper for himself.

'"Were the fields teeming with rodents?" I asked.

'"They were. The harvest machines disturbed them," he told me. "I've just come from a field where the Nusham were placing wooden stakes in the ground. The strange thing was, I caught two rats within a couple of minutes and ate them, and then I saw several mice lying dead in the nettles. Another rat appeared and I got him as well, but something seemed wrong."

'"What do you mean?" I asked.

'"Well, it all seemed too easy, catching them, I mean. So I didn't eat the last rat . . ."

'His eyes were glazed. He said he could feel a burning sensation in his stomach. Crouching and panting in the dark shadows of the tree, his body jerked as he tried to cough up a pellet. He bobbed, swivelled, stretched and twisted until finally it came out. It landed in the stubble field. The black pellet was covered with blood.

'Whispering quietly, Hoolet said: "This is the last time we'll meet, dear friend." He sat huddled on the post, the breeze ruffling his feathers.

'His body throbbed terribly as if in the clutches of a nightmare. I felt so helpless as I watched my good friend fall from the fence, turn over on to his back and flail away with his talons at some invisible enemy.

'Then the waves of death washed over him. His face folded as if in sleep. I sat silently watching his stiffening body.'

'What could it have been?' asked Kos sadly.

Barkwood explained about the poison that the Nusham laid down for rats. 'It's very dangerous for other animals and for birds too,' he said.

'Luckily the other rats weren't poisoned, otherwise I wouldn't be here now,' said Kos.

'I still miss him; he was a good friend. You can always count on me as your friend too, young Kos.'

'I know,' said Kos gratefully. 'Sometimes when I hear about these strange happenings I'm afraid.'

'That's a good thing,' said Barkwood. 'It is written in the Sacred Book of Ravens, which was inspired by the Great Eagle of Light: "We have been given the instinct of fear to make us conscious of danger, to force us to protect ourselves. All creatures must start out fearful. The youngest wild creatures must be made aware that fear keeps us safe. Only the foolhardy walk without fear."

'You must hunt for knowledge as well as food, young Kos. Well, I must be off now. I'll leave you to think about that. If you need me anytime, just call. We'll meet again. Take care!' Then he was gone over the conifers, silent as a shadow.

Kos ruffled his feathers. The story of his father's death had chilled him. He was about to leave when he noticed a mouse behind him. Barkwood, he thought, leaving food for me again. Kos quickly gulped it down and headed for home.

From a tall conifer, Barkwood watched Kos fly over the fields. For one so young to have stared into the dreadful depths of grief and loneliness and still find fun in playing shadow-games – it filled Barkwood with a warm glow.

When Kos arrived at the castle he was greeted by a most amazing sight. There was Driad, sitting on the castle wall and beside him sat the most beautiful hen barn owl. Her plumage was like the moon, silvery white with tiny specks.

'This is Snowdrop,' said Driad.

They all greeted each other with tongue-clicking and hissing.

'We met the night you stayed in the fox's hole!' continued Driad. Snowdrop gasped in surprise. 'Oh, you'd better get used to my brother Kos. He's kind of weird and has the strangest of friends!'

Kos was embarrassed, but Snowdrop blinked at him warmly.

'Well, let's go hunting before the dawn comes,' she suggested.

Snowdrop took off first into a slow, graceful flight, followed by Driad and then Kos. They caught some fieldmice in a cornfield and ate them on the nearby fence. Driad flew up, circled and hovered, dropped like a stone and caught a mouse, then flew to Snowdrop and gave a single courtship hiss. She knew the language of love. He hovered in front of her face and presented the mouse to her, which she accepted. They truly had become partners.

Kos watched Driad, who seemed dazzled by his new friend. Kos watched the wind blow through Snowdrop's light, billowing plumage, and he, too, felt new feelings which he could not explain. The three rode the air in utter silence across the dwindling night.

As the days passed, Snowdrop became very broody; she wanted to have a family of her own. Driad said they should find a suitable nesting site – maybe the old barn near the farm, or perhaps the hollow tree along the river?

'That old barn is nearly ready to collapse,' said Kos, 'There's hardly any shelter there, and the tree is used by starlings at the moment. Why don't you stay here?

It's your home as much as mine; and anyway, I'd love to help rear the young.'

'That's very kind,' said Snowdrop, 'but it will get very crowded here with owlets growing up.'

'We'll worry about that when the time comes. It's settled,' said Kos.

Driad was very pleased and proud of his little brother's generous offer. Snowdrop cheek-rubbed them both in friendship.

CHAPTER XIII

A New Family

The summer unfolded in all its beauty. The air was warm, and scented with bluebells. Everything was lush and vibrant, from the lime green of the ash leaves to the emerald green of the elm. Young birds chirped from the thickets. Every bush and tree seemed to be occupied. Young sparrowhawks called from an old magpie's nest with a hunger that never seemed to be satisfied. Both parent hawks could be seen continuously going back and forth feeding their three hungry young. There was a hum of insects in the air. Midges danced through the shafts of sunlight and serenades of songbirds filled the air.

Kos loved to sit looking out at all these things. He panted to keep cool in the warm sun. His golden-buff feathers seemed to glow in the sunlight.

Swifts screamed through the sky, the last of the migrants to arrive from Africa and the first to leave. Crag had told Kos they could sleep on the wing. A kestrel hovered in the fields. Kos wondered how it could hover for so long. Threatening rooks came, cawing loudly and dive-bombing the kestrel, who easily out-manoeuvred them in flight. Then he rose higher into the sky and disappeared on the wind.

One evening, before the sun had set, Driad appeared in a flurry of excitement at the window of the castle. He shrieked and hissed loudly. The first of five round, white eggs had hatched.

'Come on, let's go hunting!' he called to Kos.

Snowdrop would not leave the nest until all the eggs were hatched. Then she would brood them, which would take several weeks.

Driad and Kos brought food back to her. It was only then that they got to see the first arrival. It didn't look at all like an owl, its head too large for its body, its eyes closed and its skin pink. Its legs were feeble, and it had a tooth on its ivory-coloured bill that it had used for breaking through the shell.

Snowdrop seemed so happy. She crunched the eggshell with her feet and ate the pieces. It wasn't long before the eggs all hatched out. The eldest had grey-white down, the youngest looked thin and frail. Their plaintive calls demanded food constantly. Bluish eyes opened after twelve days, tiny quills

appeared and the second, thicker, white down re-
placed the thin grey. The tooth disappeared from the
bill and they were beginning now to look like owlets.

After a month the owlets' tails were growing and
they moved around the roost, bobbing about and
pouncing on feathers, or bits of bones.

They soon looked bigger than the adults and were
certainly heavier. They had plenty to eat, thanks to
Kos and Driad, who were in and out every half-hour
during the night with food for the chicks.

But the castle was becoming very crowded. The
stretching and flapping of the owlets' wings filled the
roost. Finally, Kos decided that he would leave to
roost somewhere else. It would be better for every-

one. Driad did not want Kos to leave, but he had to admit that things were cramped. Although the castle was big, it was in ruins and there were not many protected spots to roost in. Snowdrop thanked Kos and told him that she hoped he would return when the owlets had grown and moved away. The castle would be his again. Kos promised to come and visit; he felt very close to the young.

'No owlets could have been better cared for, thanks to you, Kos,' said Snowdrop. 'You're an excellent hunter!'

Kos said he was very pleased to have been able to help. Then he slipped out of the castle and stole away into the darkness.

'Good luck!' Driad and Snowdrop called after him as they watched him glide over the leafy woods.

* * *

Kos flew across the indigo sky on hushed wings. It felt good flying simply for the sake of flying. Yet there were a few nagging thoughts pulling at him. Was it wise to leave the security of the castle? Had he made too rash a judgement? It had been such fun to be part of a family. Then he scolded himself for thinking like this. He was excited and a little scared at the prospect of finding a new roost. Still, the evening was dry and warm; he could sleep anywhere!

Feeling hungry, he flew out above the fields,

quartering over the ground. Shrieking in the silent dusk, he skimmed low until he saw a shrew darting into a clump of new nettle shoots. He hovered, his beating wings giving no sound, then he pinpointed the shrew and dropped down into the nettles. Gulping it down, he flew on to the fence beside the woods and began to preen.

Eyes watched him from the woods as he ate his meal. It was his friend Crag. Sniffing the air, the fox moved cautiously towards Kos. Kos swivelled his head. 'You really know how to sneak up on someone, don't you?'

'They don't call me a crafty old fox for nothing,' said Crag. 'It's good to see you!'

'You too,' replied Kos. Then he explained about having to leave the castle.

'Why don't you come and live beside me?' suggested Crag. 'There's an oak there with a deep hole in its trunk. It would be ideal for you. It's just beside the den.'

'Great!' said Kos.

'Besides,' added Crag, 'I want to show you something very special. It's on the way to the tree.'

Through the woods they went until they came to a mound which was covered with foxgloves. There sat Asrai, surrounded by four cubs. She smiled happily at Kos.

'We have three dogs and one vixen,' said Crag

147

proudly. 'Not bad for the oldest fox in the land! They're half-grown now. Their dark brown fur is gone and they're beginning to look more like me. Of course she' – he pointed to the vixen who was pulling at a mallard wing – 'is just like her mother and has a dark belly!'

The cubs leaped around, wrestled, tumbled and tussled with each other, twisting and turning in mock battle. One of them began to chew Crag's tail, which was swinging from side to side, and bit deeply with his needle-sharp teeth. Crag yelped, and Asrai was highly amused. She scolded the cub gently, and licked Crag's face several times.

There was no need for the foxes to hunt, as the summer roadside provided fresh kills for the picking. There was lots of food strewn about outside the den – a hedgehog, a rabbit, several small birds – all the result of the previous night's road carnage.

Crag explained to Asrai that Kos had left the castle and would be staying in the oak beside old Bawson's sett near the den. Asrai was pleased that the owl would live nearby.

'There are over nine entrances to Bawson's sett,' Crag told Kos. 'He lets me use one, as you know.'

Then they set off, Crag and Kos, through the shadows of the night, until they arrived at Crag's den. Beside it stood the ancient, wizened oak tree, its twisted, leafless branches reminders of a bygone storm whose lightning had struck the very life of the tree. Kos alighted on the oak bough. My new home, he thought. He was going to enjoy it here. He gazed up at the star-studded sky.

Crag relaxed, stretched, yawned and settled himself. He sniffed the sweet-scented air, scratching his ear with his hind leg. Then he scratched behind his head, removing bits of fur in the process. Finally, he barked loudly three times, and an answering scream came across the night air from Asrai.

'We always say goodnight to each other like this,' explained Crag.

Bawson ambled out warily from the undergrowth, puffing himself up when he saw the shadow cast by Kos from the oak.

'It's okay,' said Crag, reassuringly, 'Kos here is moving in to the oak.'

'Oh, good,' said Bawson. 'A safe roost indeed. You know, I keep having dreams of rats, millions of them moving over the countryside, brown and black colours like waves over the fields.'

'It's probably because of the bad experience you had with those rats,' said Crag.

Just then a hawk-like shadow passed overhead.

'Oh, look,' said Kos, 'he's flying late – must be hungry or lost!'

Crag yelped loudly, calling 'Kuick', and the hawk-shaped bird wavered in its flight-path, then turned

back and landed on the branch beside Kos. Crag knew this stranger. It was a nightjar.

'What a pleasure to see our special visitor from Africa again!' said Crag. 'This is Bawson and Kos.'

Kos knew a lot about Africa and explained that he had made friends with a griffon vulture and two eagles who told him so many things about it.

'What are you doing in these parts?' he asked Kuick.

'Well, I'm heading home early, back to Africa. I spent many nights sitting on a rock in Wicklow singing love songs by the light of the moon, but no one heard me. I know the winds carry my song all through the quiet night. But she never came; and now the season is nearly over.'

'Don't feel too bad,' said Crag. 'You're young and there will be plenty of moonlit nights for you and your love on the heaths!'

'I hope you're right, but there are many new Nusham roosts, or houses as they call them, where we breed. I'm afraid we'll have fewer places next season and the seasons ahead.'

'Oh, don't think like that,' said Crag. 'We creatures always make out. I'm not the oldest fox in these parts for nothing, and Bawson the oldest badger – and the wisest, I may add.'

They all found comfort in the fox's words.

'I was hoping I would have the chance to say goodbye before my long flight home,' said Kuick. 'Remember the night we met?'

Crag nodded.

'It was late in the year,' the nightjar told Kos, 'the leaves were falling from the trees. I was busy hawking for moths before my journey home when I saw something shining brightly in the woods. I went to investigate, for where there is light there are moths. I found a powerful light that sent a great beam across the fields.

'As I flew to it I accidentally brushed off a Nusham sitting in the cow parsley with a death-gun. I got a terrible shock, I can tell you. Another Nusham shone the light on me. I was dazzled and faltered in the sky. I dropped to the floor of the wood and didn't move for the rest of the night.'

Then Crag continued the story. 'Actually, the Nusham were out lamping for me. I was caught in the beam and transfixed by the light. Only for Kuick here, I would certainly have been caught. You see, the light was taken off me and I ran like a hare across the fields to safety.'

'That's a wonderful story and a great start to a friendship,' said Kos, and Bawson agreed.

'Well, it wasn't quite as simple as that,' said the nightjar.

'Oh, we didn't meet until the next evening,' said Crag.

Then the nightjar, pausing briefly to snatch a passing moth, took up the story again. 'I was sitting on a mound near a clearing, looking at the stars. Everything was peaceful. I gave one burst of evening song, as I like to do, when old Jaws here pounced on me!

'He didn't make a sound and I was taken completely off-guard. Well, I thought all my nights were numbered. Then those big amber eyes stared right into me, his paw on my chest and his white teeth flashing.

'"It's you," he said, "the one who disturbed the Nusham last night." He removed his paw. "I hope I haven't hurt you," he said.

'I was minus a few breast feathers, but otherwise okay. Well, that's how we struck up a friendship. Crag spent the rest of that evening leaping into the air catching moths for me, insisting that I stay sitting on a rock, which I did. Mind you, I didn't feel very much like singing after that.

'Well, I must be away now,' said Kuick. 'Glad I met up with you. Take care, all. Oh, I forgot to tell you, I saw something very interesting when I was up near the sacred cliffs where the waves gather.'

'Don't say you saw rats!' said Bawson.

'No,' replied Kuick, 'but I saw a gathering of ravens on the cliffs. A yellowhammer told me it was an important meeting of the Council of Ravens and that they only gather at very special times on those sacred cliffs. The last meeting was during the great plague that nearly wiped out the falcons and hawks, when their eggs did not hatch and the adult birds died of the seizure and even fell from the sky or off their perches. The Nusham were to blame then, and it was only by secret invocation to the Great Eagle Spirit that the falcons were saved from extinction.

'Before that it was the great Nusham hate-war when lots of birds and wild creatures were destroyed. So this meeting must be about something either very wonderful or very dreadful. I even spotted the white-necked raven from East Africa there.'

'I wonder what all this could mean?' said Crag.

'I don't like it,' said Bawson. 'You rarely get good news anymore . . .'

It was time for the nightjar to leave. Again he made

his farewells and then, like the night, he was gone.

The blackbirds started the dawn chorus, followed by the thrushes, wrens, robins and all the summer songsters. A crescendo of notes filled the air.

CHAPTER XIV

Spies on the Wing

Thrasher scurried down the pipe to where Fericul lay, followed closely by Spike and Hack. The Emperor was sleeping soundly. They were anxious to tell him that his spies had arrived, but were afraid to awaken him. Sniffing nervously, they decided Thrasher should do it, as he had brought the Emperor a box of apples the previous day, pleasing him greatly. The remains of unfinished apples were strewn around the bed of straw.

Thrasher gently whispered in Fericul's ear. Not a move! Thrasher stroked him lightly with his paw. The Emperor sprang up and knocked Thrasher to the ground, his heavy frame pinning the helpless rat.

'Don't ever wake me again unless I order you to! Do you hear me?' he roared.

'Yes,' stuttered Thrasher, and he backed away from the Emperor's contemptuous eyes.

Hack called out nervously. 'But you d . . did, Your Highness. You did ask us to tell you the moment your spies arrived, and they have.'

The Emperor relaxed. 'Forgive me, Thrasher, I have so much to think of, and I need my rest. I have the responsibility of all the rodent population on my shoulders; it's a heavy burden. You must realise this.'

'Oh, we do!' they answered in unison.

'Good, my comrades. You are loyal and faithful. Soon you will all benefit greatly. Now, go tell my spies to wait outside the tip. I don't want the others finding out my business just yet. They will be informed soon enough. Go, I will be with you shortly.'

They hurried away, eager to obey his every command, for they knew how quickly his black anger could be aroused if they didn't. They had all witnessed his murderous rage.

The drone of bluebottles filled the air. Cars could be heard in the distance leaving the city dump and heading down the dirt road on the outskirts of the fields. A dusty cloud rose from the ground, covering the hedgerows.

Hack scurried over the fields, stopping briefly to sniff the air and check the sky for hovering kestrels. Thrasher gave him a friendly glance, his eyes thanking him for stepping in to defuse the situation with the Emperor.

Two hooded crows, Skiter and Whizzer, the Emperor's spies, flew ahead. In a quiet section of an abandoned field they all sat waiting for Fericul. The 'hoodies', as they were called, perched upon a shattered tree trunk recently hacked down by a Nusham machine, the sap still sticky in its splintered centre. An uneasy alliance existed between the rats and the crows.

There was a long silence, as the grim-faced hoodies watched from their vantage point for their beloved Emperor. Finally Hack broke the silence by asking the hoodies how they came to be in his service. Whizzer and Skiter looked at each other as if deciding whether to tell or not. Then Whizzer explained how they had been abandoned after the tree they had been nesting in was felled.

'A large rat – Rattus – happened to find us. Instead of trying to kill us he fed us, bringing food and shelter, and protecting us from dangers. Rattus is a loyal servant to the Emperor; it was he who found the ancient place that you rodents call RATLAND. He made us swear allegiance to the Emperor who would come from foreign places to protect us through a future holocaust that would destroy many wild creatures.

'That's why we've thrown in our lot with your kind. We believe that your race will conquer the earth. But we have been chosen for the most important mission of all, to help make the great dream a reality for the mighty Fericul!'

Skiter added solemnly: 'All creatures must work together to fulfil the Emperor's dream.'

The rats looked at each other. They did not tell the hoodies that Rattus was a traitor who'd had his throat torn out and whose skull was to be used as a footstool for the Emperor's throne.

Suddenly, Fericul lurched out from the tangled briars and hurled himself between the crows and the rats. They were all taken completely by surprise. There was an edge of tension; had the Emperor been listening to the conversation, or had he just arrived?

'Cat-napping?' said Fericul with a mocking grin. He

could see they were all startled. 'Vigilance, stealth and cunning, my comrades, at all times, that is the way we will survive, destroy our enemies, and thrive. Remember that. In life, comrades, you have to dig in, and maintain your position.' He seemed to relax, scratching a bit and checking his long tail.

Then he summoned the crows to the ground and stared hard into their eyes. 'Have you anything to report to me?' he whispered.

The hoodies hesitated. 'We visited every rookery in the area,' they said finally. 'Naturally, we couldn't get too close to any of them, but, from speaking to a couple of jackdaws, we think it's the rookery near the big house that's the oldest. It had been deserted for some time, but in recent years a rook named Shimmer arrived there and started a colony.'

'Shimmer?' said the Emperor. 'No, that's not the name I was told of. Are you sure he is the one who started the rookery?'

'Shimmer is only a nickname,' continued Skiter. 'His real name is Meldeck!'

'Meldeck! Yes!' said the Emperor gleefully. 'Meldeck! Follow him, he will lead us to it. Keep an eye on him from dawn to dusk. He is the keeper!'

The keeper of what? wondered the rats. The hoodies appeared to know. Then Fericul looked at Spike, Thrasher and Hack. 'All will be revealed soon, my comrades.'

* * *

Whizzer and Skiter watched Shimmer for several weeks. They saw the rooks build new nests in the elms, adding to the great rookery. They watched food being brought to the hungry young. They saw the fledglings grow big and strong.

All this time Shimmer acted and behaved just like the other rooks. Whizzer and Skiter were wondering whether, in fact, they were looking at the wrong rookery, but they continued their surveillance, for they knew how important their mission was, and the Emperor would not tolerate failure.

One bright, clear morning, before the rookery was stirring, a lone rook flew quietly over the elms, unaware that eyes watched him from a nearby tree. The two hoodies, skulking in a nearby horse-chestnut, watched as he inked across the fire-dazzled sunrise.

The hoodies, equally powerful flyers, took to the air on determined wings, keeping their distance, but making sure that Shimmer was never out of sight.

Across the river he flew, while below him twittering swallows were flying low over the water, displaying their acrobatic skills. The sunlight danced on a brown, meandering river. Cattle grazed in fields of clover and buttercups, swishing their tails.

A kestrel hovered, tail fanned, slowly falling as if being unwound by some invisible thread, then dropped like a stone to the ground, at the last minute pulling out from his swoop to resume hovering in a different part of the field.

The hedgerows were now alive with birdsong. A flycatcher fanned into the air from a fence to catch a buzzing insect. The slow-moving figure of Shimmer seemed oblivious to these early-morning activities. He floated on past white, fluffy clouds in the blue sky, concentrating on his task.

It was a great honour and he felt very privileged, but he also felt the weight of the responsibility he must shoulder. The summer solstice approached and the Council would be meeting. How could he have known, when he established a rookery in the old elms, that the old trees held such a treasure? Now that the elms were cursed by the mysterious malady, he felt sure the Council would approve of his secret hiding place in an ancient circular tower which had been used by the peaceful Nusham to store their sacred objects so many solstices ago, when oaks were plentiful.

Skiter and Whizzer were hungry and weary. They hoped this old rook would rest a while, but instead his pace had quickened.

His flight had not faltered since he set out on the journey. As he approached the grey-green, lichen-covered trees, Shimmer could see the tower standing tall over the dark yews. He alighted on a leaning headstone, dressed with yellow-white lichen.

Sitting silently, his beautiful black plumage gleaming in the sunlight, he looked cautiously around.

Some jackdaws flew by. Shimmer waited. No one must see him enter the tower. He preened. It was so peaceful here compared to the bustle and noise of the rookery. Not that he resented that; he loved to see new life coming into the world, but the clamour of spring was a bit of a strain on his old ears. He was rarely alone, even when he went to feed. Yet, when he thought of the rooks moving in unison across the warm evening sky before settling down to roost, he felt very proud.

All seemed quiet now. Looking around once more, he flew to the top of the tower and circled several times before alighting on the window sill. This was a ritual whose meaning was known only to the Council of Ravens and a few of the older rooks.

Looking behind him once more, he went inside. It was a cold, hollow tower. He flew to the carved, wooden casket. This was always the most anxious moment, and the most exciting. He trembled. Then, he prised the casket open by wedging his strong grey bill between the lid and the box.

As the lid flipped back, a yellow-gold glow filled the tower with shafts of delicate light. The colours throbbed as Shimmer peered into the box, knowing all was well. The dazzling light made him blink. His plumage gleamed, bathed in the golden light. Every time he opened the casket the same feeling of awe overcame him.

The Sacred Feather had strong magical properties and he could feel its healing rays course through his body. The power was at its strongest during the summer and winter solstices.

Since it had come into his possession Shimmer had never exploited the power of the Feather. The Council of Ravens were the ones who would know how to use it wisely.

As long as it remained with the birds, it would protect all creatures of the sky world, the earth world and the water world. But if it were ever used with the wrong motives, it could destroy everything. A catastrophe so great would occur that all the birds would fall from the sky and the wild creatures would disappear from the earth, according to the Book of Ravens.

Shimmer knew this to be true. He also knew that their world was in more danger than ever before. He didn't mean the traps or deadly guns; these were things that they somehow managed to live with. It was the other strange ways of Nusham that worried him.

He had witnessed and heard of so many meaningless and cruel deeds: the poisoning of the rivers and lakes, and the upturned fish in their thousands, as far as the eye could see, lying white-bellied, gasping their last breath; the nesting trees hacked down; the burning of forests, the black clouds of death that burned the eyes if you flew through them; the poisoning of insects, crops, land and sea.

Shimmer shuddered just thinking about it. Then he wondered was that the reason that the Sacred Feather had been rediscovered after being lost in the mists of time. So many creatures did not know about or believe in the old laws and writings of the Book of Ravens. Yet here he had the Feather to prove it. Did it matter, he thought, as long as a few believed and knew the truth?

Shimmer's thoughts brought him back to the time when he first came across the precious object. It all seemed so far away now, such a long time ago, yet it was as clear in his mind as if it had happened yesterday.

* * *

The young Shimmer had left the security of the large rookery where he had lived because his father's dying words had told him to establish a new rookery. Why me? Shimmer had thought. He was happy and content living in the place where he had been born. There were still plenty of places to build new homes in the branches of the elms that grew so close together. But he could not refuse his father, Greypeck's, wishes.

'You will know the right place, the right trees, where you should build the new rookery,' said Greypeck. 'I have seen it all in a vision. There is a light there, a special light . . .' That was all he said before stealing away on the wings of Deva.

And so, on the evening of Greypeck's death, Shimmer said goodbye to family and friends, took off and went questing for the tree of light. How do you find a tree of light? he wondered. Was it a sycamore, an elm, oak or ash?

When Shimmer asked one of the oldest and wisest rooks about a tree of light, he was told: 'All trees have the light within, otherwise they would die . . .' This might be true, but it wasn't the answer he was looking for. There must be a tree somewhere which had a special light shining from it.

He had set out on a long, difficult and lonely journey, he realised. He was chased out of some places by other established rook colonies and was nearly shot out of the sky by a Nusham with a death-gun. He brooded long and hard on his father's words and visions. How could he fulfil those dreams?

One day during a terrible storm, when the clouds loomed grey and forbidding and the rumble and claps of thunder and luminous streaks of lightning crossed the sky followed by sheets of rain, Shimmer needed to find shelter quickly. Up ahead he spotted a cluster of elms which seemed to beckon. Suddenly, as he winged his way towards them, a jagged streak of lightning struck the centre elm, shearing a large branch clean off. Wavering in his flight, a nervous twinge ran through his body.

His anxious gaze noticed light emanating from the tree whose branch had been severed moments earlier – a single shaft of warm yellow light! This was it – the tree of light – just as his father had seen in a vision.

The terrible sense of foreboding was gone; Shimmer was awestruck. The thunder stopped, the rain ceased, and tranquillity descended – the golden light after the storm. His feelings were in turmoil. He felt invincible and the world seemed timeless. His wings floated towards the light. Alighting on the bare branches of the ancient elm, he peered into the gaping hole. There it was – a magical Feather that showered him with light! He didn't know at the time that it was the Sacred Feather from the Eagle of Light. But he did know it was a precious talisman. On closer examination he could see that the broken bough had revealed a hole hewn out of the tree trunk, a hole designed to keep the Feather carefully hidden.

Who else had witnessed this wondrous event? he wondered. He decided to hide the Feather until he knew what to do with it. He quickly tore chunks of bark from a fallen branch and covered the Feather with them, encasing the light once more.

Later, he sought advice from one of the rook elders who told him to go to the cliffs where the waves gather to meet with the Council of Ravens and report everything, which he did. They were filled with a great joy, for the predictions of the Sacred Book of the Ravens had been fulfilled.

Young Shimmer was made Keeper of the Feather until the Council of Ravens would meet. They could not tell him when this was to be.

In the spring of the following year he had started the new rookery, building the first nest directly above the hole, by pulling twigs off the live elms. His father had once told him never to use dead twigs because they were too brittle.

It wasn't long before rooks came from far and near to form the finest rookery in the land and before the breeding season had begun fully that year, Shimmer had removed the Feather to the tower with its secret chambers. He was amused upon his return to hear the rooks talking about some magpies who said that they had witnessed two suns shining in the sky on that day. None of the rooks believed them. Shimmer had remained silent, grateful that the light had blotted out his image as he carried the Sacred Feather across the sky.

* * *

As it was now over four summers and winters since Shimmer had spoken to the Council, he felt sure that the time must be ripe for that meeting, for all life was now being tested. The future itself seemed to be at risk. He was so lost in these silent reflections that he did not notice that most of the day had already passed. Closing the casket gently, he felt relieved to know that the Feather was safe.

Moving to the window he peered out to make sure the coast was clear. On the ground below, young robins with speckled breasts hopped about, unaware of the dark shadow passing over them.

Shimmer's flight was more relaxed on the return journey, his senses heightened. He felt at one with the world, like a young rook again. This happened

each time he visited the Sacred Feather. Its aura of mystery was the source of life; he knew this.

On he flew, through the windless air, carrying an immense peacefulness within. The countryside looked lush. Several rooks came to greet him as he neared his home, for they had seen him cross the fields. The sun's last light flooded the sky as Shimmer joined the clamouring rooks on their sunset flight before roosting.

Two hooded crows flew towards the stone tower.

CHAPTER XV

New Home – New Dangers

Kos had made several trips to the castle to see the young owlets, now almost fully fledged. They spent most of the time flapping their wings, preening, taking short flights around the castle, and sometimes flying across to the trees and back to the broken castle walls. Driad and Snowdrop were still feeding them. The owlets' facial discs were well-defined now, with dark reddish-brown at the corners of their black eyes. Kos was amused at their raucous calls: the constant wailing, hissing, snoring, squeaking, chirping, screeching, yelling.

One looked so like Snowdrop it was uncanny. The rest bore a close resemblance to Driad. And Kos was pleased to notice that the one called Hoolet, named after their grandfather, had white primary feathers and a white tail just like himself.

The owlets were always glad to see Kos. Occasionally they would land on his back, making him almost
lose his balance. When he came visiting he would
catch food with Driad and Snowdrop for the owlets
– and they seemed to be permanently hungry.

Kos missed the security of the castle walls, yet he
saw and heard a lot more of the inhabitants of the
woods from the oak tree. There was so much to see
and enjoy. The medley of summer sounds – the wood
pigeons cooing in the trees, the dunnock picking
through the mossy branches collecting billfuls of
insects, the blackbirds moving under the bracken, the
bird-nest orchid which grew under the beech, the
butterflies and rabbits, old Bawson raiding a wasps'
nest, his long snout tucking into its centre and the
frantic wasps unable to sting through his bristly coat,
the spotted flycatcher showing her young how to take
advantage of Bawson's activity by fanning out from
the perch, catching a wasp and removing the sting
before eating it. There was always something to see
in this emerald cathedral.

One evening, on his way to the castle, Kos was
spotted by the two hoodies, Skiter and Whizzer. They
flew after him with strong wingbeats, cawing loudly.
One swooped down and jabbed so hard with his beak
that Kos nearly fell from the sky. He faltered, then
flapped, trying hard to escape. Another jab from a

beak sent small feathers floating in the air. Kos shrieked and turned his body to kick out at them. He flung himself to the ground and raked at the hoodies, who were quick to avoid his sharp talons. They continued to peck at him from both sides.

Kos couldn't understand their attitude; he wasn't touching them, so why attack him? There was plenty of room in the sky.

Still they hammered blows to his body with sharp beaks. Try as he would, he couldn't shake off these bullies.

'Leave him be!' shouted someone in a loud voice.

The hoodies stopped to see who was giving them orders. There stood Shimmer and seven other rooks who had witnessed the attack from a field and flown over to investigate.

Skiter was about to continue his bill-stabbing, when Shimmer called sharply again: 'I said leave him alone!'

'Whose side are you on?' Skiter called back angrily. 'He's an owl after all, or have you forgotten?'

'I know what an owl is and this one is my friend, understand?' retorted Shimmer.

Kos lay still as the hoodies pointed out that in their law owls were sworn enemies.

'Don't tell me the law,' said Shimmer. 'In the Sacred Book of Ravens it says that all creatures must strive to live in peace and harmony. Now, clear off, you lot!'

'This will be reported to the Council of Ravens,' said

Skiter. 'You'll be punished. We promise!' And they flew off in high dudgeon.

'Are you all right, my friend?' Shimmer asked Kos when the hoodies had gone.

'Yes, I think so,' said Kos. 'I'm really glad you turned up, but I hope you won't get into trouble for it.'

'Don't worry about me,' said Shimmer. 'I'm too old a crow to worry about two upstarts like that!'

Suddenly, one of the rooks shouted: 'A fox!' and flew away into the sky.

Shimmer turned around: 'Hello, Crag. Still able to sneak up on my kind?'

'Oh, you know me, Shimmer, it's in my nature!' Crag turned to Kos who was checking his feathers. 'Well, more trouble, I see! You know, Shimmer, things are never dull with young Kos around!'

'That's for sure,' said Shimmer. 'Well, I'm off!' and he took to the sky.

'I don't know how to repay Shimmer and yourself for all your help,' said Kos.

'Oh, you bring out the best in us,' said Crag.

'And the worst in the hoodies!' added Kos.

*   *   *

The evening brought great joyous relief – and the sight of Driad's entire family all flying in the starry sky to visit Kos in his home in the tree. Kos greeted them with a long shriek, and they hissed back. The owlets had come to say goodbye. After twelve weeks they were fully grown – flying over fields, flapping, hovering and catching their own food. They had learnt well.

Snowdrop knew it was time to let them go, but a feeling of both joy and sadness welled up inside her. They all sat together on a fence for a long time.

Then slowly, one by one, the young ones departed, elegantly gliding and fluttering over the fields into the still night.

'I wish them every success in the breeding years ahead,' said Driad, 'but I can't help being worried. You know, it's getting more and more difficult to find suitable roosting and nesting places. The Nusham cut down the trees that don't produce summer leaves, then they burn them.'

'The falcons and hawks are affected too,' added Snowdrop. 'The old barns are disappearing and the new ones don't give enough cover for nesting. Of course, they're still worth a visit for the rats who feed there.'

Kos said that he had heard from old Crag that some Nusham were actually putting up wooden nest-boxes in the new barns especially for owls.

'Oh, I hope that's true,' said Snowdrop, 'it would be wonderful!'

'There must be a catch,' said Driad suspiciously.

'Why would Nusham help us?'

'Perhaps not all Nusham are cruel. Maybe some even love trees, birds and animals,' insisted Kos, although his own experiences of Nusham had been anything but friendly.

Driad gave a far-carrying farewell shriek, and then, without a word, he and Snowdrop left for the castle.

Kos sat alone and preened a little, ruffling his feathers which then fell back neatly along his body.

Crag came by for a late evening chat. 'A fine family indeed,' said Crag. 'May they fly for many nights on silent wings. My cubs are all grown up too and have moved away to new territories.'

'That's what it's all about,' said Kos.

'This might be my last breeding season,' said Crag, with some regret.

'Why?' asked Kos.

'Well, recently I've been having strange dreams – Nusham coming after me with horses and hounds. I run with all my might to escape them. Asrai calls to me, the sky is blood-red as are the clothes of the Nusham. I run and run, heavy hooves behind me, hounds baying for blood – mine – my body racked with pain. Run, faster, faster I keep telling myself, my throat burning. But they're gaining on me, closer, closer, no place to hide, closing in on me, teeth gnashing.' Crag became silent as these thoughts coursed through his mind.

'Then?' asked Kos. 'What happens next?'

'I wake up!' said Crag, with a wry smile.

'Wow!' said Kos. 'That's not a dream, it's a nightmare. I felt scared just listening to it, but the Nusham don't do that kind of thing, do they?'

Crag did not reply.

'Horses wouldn't agree to do that,' insisted Kos.

'They have no choice,' said Crag. 'If they don't, they get whipped. I've heard the horses talk in the fields when things are quiet. They don't enjoy it. I've seen horses trying to leap over a hedgerow with a ditch on the far side, then crash down on to the hard ground. If they're injured they're taken away and never seen again.

'But the hounds enjoy the chase. They won't stop until they get one of us. Sometimes the Nusham come around the day before and block all the entrances to the dens so we can't go to ground.

'Bawson even had his sett blocked once. It took him days to clear the entrances again.'

With that, Bawson appeared from the undergrowth. He dropped a black rat between Kos and Crag.

'Look . . .' he said nervously. 'See . . .' They both looked puzzled. 'A black rat! They belong in the cities, not here in the fields. There's something going on, I tell you. I found this one raiding some nests for young birds. Where there is one, there are more!'

'A raiding party to the farms,' said Crag. 'Don't

alarm yourself too much. Besides, they taste just as nice as the brown ones!'

'If the Nusham discover black rats in the area they will lay their poison and we'll all suffer,' said Bawson.

'They do that anyway,' said Crag, 'and it hasn't killed us yet!'

'I'd just like to know what's going on in my territory,' continued Bawson, 'that's all. I'm not over-reacting, am I?'

'No,' said Crag, 'you're right to be cautious. We're all pleased you're so thorough and wary.'

'I'm glad you understand,' said Bawson. 'It's not only for myself I get worried, it's for everybody. Well, I'd better turn in. You're well, Kos?'

'Yes,' came the reply.

'Good, that's very good. Well, goodnight. Oh, by the way, Crag, I've been having bad dreams about horses and hounds.'

'Well, I suppose I'm in those dreams?' said Crag.

'Yes, I'm afraid you are. They're very, very vague. I can see you being taken on a long journey.'

'Well, Bawson, next time you dream, leave me out of it!' said Crag, and they all laughed.

Then Bawson shuffled off into the darkness and Crag went to ground.

Kos sat for a while on his tree, looking at the night sky. His mind floated in silent thought, thinking of Crag, Bawson, Barkwood, Driad, Snowdrop, Asrai and the young owlets and foxes.

Was it all chance that their lives should have become so entwined, or was there some plan older than the stars, forging their lives so that they should all meet now at this exact time in the seasons of life?

The first leaves of the horse-chestnut tree began to fall. Kos watched as they came twisting and winding to the ground.

CHAPTER XVI

Death on the Wind

Autumn descended on the woods. The trees were veiled in scarlet, orange and pale gold and the green of the bracken bed turned to copper brown. The winds sent the leaves reeling through the air, snapping brittle ferns as they passed by. Berries filled the hedgerows and the birds gathered together in large flocks ready to leave. The morning light revealed pearls of dew on the cobwebs as they lay like nets over the stubble in the fields.

One chilly morning Crag hurried up from his den. He sniffed the air nervously. There was a silence, almost menacing in its stillness.

Kos, too, peered out from his dwelling in the oak tree and Bawson came from his sett. They all felt uneasy.

'Can you see anything?' said Crag to Kos.

Kos looked across the fields. Nothing strange as far as he could see. All seemed quiet.

Then they heard it – the baying of hounds!

Wood pigeons in clapping flight hurried from the fields. Rooks called noisily in alarm. A stoat dropped the blackbird he had just killed and ran for cover. Rabbits scurried to their warren. Greenfinches and linnets circled in fear.

Faint and far-off came the sound of a horn. Crag peered through the hedge. In the distance he could see the menacing hounds baying and milling over the fields, followed by the hunters on horseback – and then . . . a fox running flat out, tail flying in the wind.

The pack was close behind it. Barkwood, the long-eared owl, flew over and alighted beside Kos, his orange eyes blinking anxiously.

'It's Asrai!' he screamed. 'They're after her!'

For a moment Crag was numbed, then, quickly recovering, he bolted through the hedgerow and away across the fields.

Now he could see that Asrai was weakening. A sick feeling of fear filled his mind. Why was she running up-wind and allowing the dogs to follow her scent? Then he understood – she was deliberately trying to lead the hounds away from the area where she knew her offspring still banded together. He must try and divert them.

On and on she ran, her mud-covered body tired, her mouth open gasping for breath, her tongue hanging. She faltered several times, then surged on in her race for life. The excited hounds streamed across the land hard on her heels. The horses galloped, the drumming of hooves sending terror through the exhausted fox. They jumped over ditches and fences; on and on they pushed, clambering over field, ditch and hedgerow. One Nusham fell to the ground and his horse ran free.

Asrai was now running like a beaten fox. Her throat burned and her legs were numb.

Kos flew from his perch across the fields. Barkwood and Bawson shouted to him to come back, there was nothing he could do.

From above, Kos saw Crag run across the oncoming hounds. Nusham shouted, hounds barked and bayed, and Kos shrieked a piercing shriek – but no one noticed him. The hounds divided into two groups.

Kos alighted on an ash tree and watched the hounds disappear to the right and to the left over a

ridge, the horses, now also divided in two, close behind at full gallop, sending clouds of fallen leaves into the air.

From the safety of the woods and long grasses all eyes were riveted on the spectacle. The sound of the hunting horn carried on the wind – and the heavy scent of fox permeated the air.

Then came an uneasy quietness, followed by soft, twittering conversation from the hedgerows. Horses and hounds seemed to disappear like apparitions.

A kestrel moved cautiously in the air and circled, searching the ground meticulously. Then she shook the wind from her wings and dropped into the field, mantled her catch, and flew away. Her appearance seemed to bring a sense of calmness and normality as she hovered over the next field.

Kos waited and watched. He stayed there all day hoping to see his friends Crag and Asrai. The light faded and dusk came flooding in. Then Kos flew silently over the fields to where he had last seen the foxes, hounds and horses.

Everything seemed very quiet after such pandemonium. But Kos felt a terrible sense of foreboding. The smell of death hung in the air.

Ever alert, he circled the long grasses. Tilting his wings, he dipped lower, his black eyes scanning for any sign of Crag or Asrai. He moved over the contours of the ground, passing the cow parsley at the edge of the woods – and finally he saw the crushed nettles. He landed on a rough ditch nearby.

Here in the flattened nettles a terrible thing had happened. All Kos could see were the remains of the slaughter. A trail of blood across some matted leaves on the dark, damp soil and torn pieces of chestnut fur were all that remained of Asrai's body.

Kos gave a hellish shriek into the night air. Then came another shriek as if to lay bare all his misery.

But where was Crag?

CHAPTER XVII

The Black Stranger

Crag never returned. News came from Sheila, the heron, that he had suffered the same fate as Asrai, but nobody found his body. Kos stayed in his roost for several days, too sad to venture out.

Finally, he looked out one morning. He had heard the plaintive cries of the lapwings – 'pee-weet, pee-weet' – their melancholy tones ringing through the silence. Through the half-light of the morning, he watched the lapwings' lazy flight, then their tumble from the sky as if mortally wounded. Twisting and turning and finally resting in the stubble fields, they searched for grubs and beetles, but were forever alert and watchful.

Swallows were gathering in flocks, ready to migrate. For some it was a journey they had made

several times; for others it was their first time to fly across the most hazardous terrain known to birds to winter in the warm suns of Africa. Most of the other migrant songsters were stocking up on food to make that same arduous journey.

The morning dew lingered for a time on the grasses before the pale, ascending sun misted it away. A harvestman scanned the soil in search of small insects, at the same time keeping a careful lookout for his deadly enemy, the centipede, who was always keen to make a meal out of him.

Kos breathed in the fresh morning air. He watched the antics of the squirrels as they made their way through the twisting branches of the beech tree, running down the bark, searching among the fallen leaves on the wood floor for beechnuts and chestnuts. He saw one squirrel break through the prickly seedcase of the chestnut, revealing its shiny brown nut.

Their jerky, erratic movement and flicking tail revealed their nervous disposition. At the slightest hint of danger they would freeze their bodies, then quickly scurry up the nearest tree to the safety of their drey.

Kos took off into the sky, his body flashing white against the deep morning blue. Below him, a jay, who was burying acorns, rattled in annoyance. An alarmed songthrush flew into the hedge. Kos could feel the nip in the air as he winged his way over the trees. He decided to call on Old Bawson to see how he was.

He hissed several times at the different entrances to the sett, but there was no answer. Remembering that Crag had said Old Bawson was getting deaf, he shrieked down the tunnels, hoping the sound would reach the resting-chambers. But there was still no reply. He waited several moments, preened a little, then was away again on hushed wings.

Perhaps Barkwood might know where Bawson was; he very much hoped so. Anyway, it would be good to talk to a friend.

A liquid light washed over the trees. Kos circled the mighty, silent beech grove, which was cowled in shadows, then flew across the stream that trickled through the woods where he found Barkwood sleeping, his body pressed up against a tall fir tree.

As Kos alighted on the same branch the old owl blinked one orange eye open.

'Oh, welcome, Kos, it's good to see you again. Terrible news about Crag and Asrai.'

'The place won't be the same without them,' said Kos.

'And have you heard about Shimmer?' asked
Barkwood. 'He's in serious trouble. I overheard two magpies talking about it here yesterday. He was reported to the Council of Ravens of the Sacred Cliffs. His crime is so bad, they said, that he may have sounded his own death knell.'

Kos was shocked. 'Oh no!' he cried. 'That's because of me. You see, he saved me from two hooded crows.'

'Calm down,' said Barkwood. 'That's not it at all. It's because a sacred relic was stolen and Shimmer was the custodian of it.'

'What? A relic? I never heard of that.'

'Well, the crows believe they have an actual feather from the Eagle of Light. And it has magical powers. Apparently, down through the ages, it has been passed around to different bird species to hold for a breeding season. It brings power, strength and good luck to those who believe and accept its sacredness. And it seems that the birds who have rejected it, or don't believe in its powers, become extinct. They lose their protection and eventually the Nusham destroy them, either deliberately or in ignorance, I don't know.

'My father spoke of the Feather many times when we were young. He told me that when the Eagle of Light created all things, he told the birds he would give them a gift to remember him by. They must use it wisely so that all wild creatures would benefit from it. But it must always remain in the possession of the birds. When it had passed to all the families of birds in the world then it must return to the Sacred Cliffs.

'He then scraped the code of life for all to see on the Cliffs, before returning to the higher sky. Oddly, the Feather got lost through the ages, and it entered into the realms of fantasy and birdlore. It was Shimmer who discovered it in the legendary rook colony of Croker. That's where old Shimmer set up his first nesting colony. Now he's under rookery arrest.'

'He never told me about all this,' said Kos.

'It was a secret. You see, Shimmer was guarding the Feather until the next Council of Ravens. Then he was going to take it to them and they would decide who should have it next. But now it's gone. And the worst part is, according to the magpies, the Feather must be returned before the winter solstice. If it isn't, then all the birds will fall from the sky, never to fly again!'

'How can they know this?' asked Kos.

'They say it's foretold in the Book of Ravens,' answered Barkwood.

'What will the Council do to Shimmer?' inquired Kos.

'He'll be tried. They'll vote on how severe the punishment should be. I'm afraid they won't be easy on him. This is the worst crime of all!'

'We must help him,' said Kos. 'What can we do?'

'He's beyond help now. The rumours have spread rapidly throughout the woods about Shimmer.'

*　　*　　*

Rooks circled silently over the tree where Shimmer was held, guarding him closely. Shimmer sat, silently awaiting his fate. Even his relations in the rookery had turned against him, the shame and fear was so awesome. Four magpies sat above him, scolding and jeering. Shimmer had never allowed magpies near the rookery, as they were not to be trusted, especially during the breeding season, but now he had to sit quietly and suffer their insults.

He knew he deserved to be punished for allowing the Feather to be stolen, but what gnawed at his mind was: who had taken it, and for what reason?

It was a mystery he would like to solve, but it looked like he would never get the chance. The previous day he had tried to escape, to see if he could locate the precious Feather, but this was taken as an attempt to escape his punishment. He was knocked to the ground and beaten by the young, aggressive rooks, who gashed his forehead and punctured his side. Even his tail feathers, of which he took so much care, were badly broken. He hadn't the heart to fight back; these were his own kind, nephews and cousins.

'Bad luck will follow us because of you!' said one rook angrily. 'The day of destruction is coming – we're cursed!' This brought a frenzy of fear and panic, and they called out harshly, swooping at Shimmer, ready to kill him.

'Stop!' an old rook shouted loudly. 'We must do this according to the law, lest we all face the Council of Ravens!'

This quietened the young ones down somewhat, for they were in awe of the Council of Ravens.

Then the jays, who were normally so secretive, started to circle the sky.

'He's coming!' they shouted.

The jackdaws added their voices, proclaiming his arrival in even louder tones.

A dark, mysterious shape flew across the sky. The ragged wing-tip moved slowly against the magenta, vermillion and lemon light of evening. The sun seemed flattened into an oval shape, as the menacing black figure passed by, with inquisitive eyes watching its every beat.

There was no mistaking the strong flight and

wedge-shaped tail of the raven. No creature would have changed places with Shimmer, not for anything. The birds cowered as he passed over. In a deep, croaking call, the raven announced his presence. The others knew only too well that he had arrived. A reception committee of rooks, hoodies and magpies flew out to greet him.

'Welcome, Your Excellency, Your Most Gracious Highness. It is indeed a great honour you bestow upon us by your visit to our humble abode!'

The raven flew through them, brushing them to either side. They had to flap hard to keep pace with him.

'Are you hungry, Your Excellency? You must be tired after your long journey.'

The raven's fierce expression made them flinch.

'This is not a social visit, but an official one,' he snapped grimly. 'Perhaps you do not know how serious this matter is?' The words seemed to spit from his powerful bill.

They were silent.

'Well, let's get on with it,' he said.

Barkwood and Kos watched thousands of rooks and crows glide and circle in the sky, emitting loud cries. Then they set off, shrouding the sky like black spectres, Shimmer hidden somewhere in their midst. It was impossible to tell which was Shimmer, but the raven stood out clearly against the masses of crows as he led them towards the Sacred Cliffs.

It was a very impressive sight, thought the two owls, if only poor Shimmer hadn't been the reason for it all. Finally, the rooks disappeared from view and an uneasy silence returned to the area. Woodpigeons flew to the fields, and rabbits sniffed the air as they emerged slowly from their warrens. A robin sang his melancholy song from a bare hawthorn branch.

'What can be done for Shimmer?' asked Kos.

'Nothing, I'm afraid,' said Barkwood. 'Unless, of course, you find the Feather.'

'You're right, that's it! Find the Feather. Well, there's no time to waste, I'm off!' Kos launched himself from the tree and glided over the woods.

'Good luck!' shouted Barkwood.

* * *

Fericul had just finished a meal of feral pigeon when he noticed the two hoodies sitting on the pylons near the dump. He turned to Spike, Hack and Thrasher.

'They're here . . .' he whispered.

Other rats were scurrying about, nibbling through black refuse bags and searching their contents.

'Wait here. Make sure no one follows me.'

The Emperor slipped quietly through the mounds of rubbish until he came to Skiter and Whizzer. He squealed and the two hoodies alighted beside him. 'Well, what news? I hope it's good – good for me, that is.' The Emperor's eyes burned with excited anticipation, dry blood caking his face from gorging on the pigeon.

'Oh, great news. Everything went according to plan. We got the Sacred Feather and brought it to the chamber as requested.'

Fericul laughed a demonic laugh. 'Excellent, my true and loyal servants. You will be rewarded for this great work!' Then, staring hard into their eyes, he asked about Shimmer.

'He has been arrested and is to be tried by the Council of Ravens,' said Whizzer.

'This will send shock waves throughout the bird world, and sound the death knell for all who do not follow Your Highness,' added Skiter.

'Everything is falling into place. Now go to the Sacred Cliffs, watch the trial and come back and tell me all about it, every last detail. And bring me the skull of Shimmer. I want it for RATLAND! Now, away! Make haste. You have done a great service that will not be forgotten. Your names will be carved on the walls of RATLAND above my throne!'

The two hoodies took flight, giving a triple 'ka-ka' call in salute as they left.

Hack, Spike and Thrasher sat patiently awaiting the Emperor's return. Then they spotted him moving sluggishly over the ground, gulls circling and screaming above him. They watched him approach, their eyes darting about fearfully. He gave no indication of his mood. When he finally stood close beside them, his face had a grave-like stillness. This made them even more fearful.

A sly grin broke slowly across his face and his eyes gleamed.

'My comrades, we are now the proud owners of the Sacred Feather!' he announced. They cheered loudly. 'Tonight we leave for RATLAND, our ancestral home. Spread the word, comrades, squeal our message far and wide. Soon we will be invincible!'

His teeth gleamed in the fading light, then, with his mind and hunger appeased, he rested, lying across a tyre like a bloated leech, sleeping soundly.

Hack, Spike and Thrasher left to pass on the news of the midnight departure, squealing the message through the clear night. The word spread quickly from rodent to rodent: We move tonight on the midnight hour . . . destination – RATLAND!

CHAPTER XVIII

Journey into Ratland

Kos skirted across the black water of the lake, which was broken only by the gleaming wavelets that the night winds stirred up, then he flew over the stark, dark bog. Mist began to rise and spread out over the heathers and grasses.

He had been on the wing for hours, searching near the big house, then along the river banks, in and out through the woods, over the meadows, scanning the hedgerows and the farmyard, searching every nook and cranny for the Sacred Feather.

Kos was hungry. He was amazed that in all his probing of the night, he had not yet seen one rat, mouse or shrew. On and on he flapped and glided through the night air. He could feel the chill of the wind rise under his wings, and his body ached with

tiredness. Yet his friendship with Shimmer spurred him on. He owed it to him. He had lost so many real friends, and didn't want to lose any more.

If only Crag were here! He would surely have found the Sacred Feather by now. But who would want to take it? Kos wondered. If it were the Nusham, he would have no chance of recovering it.

He thought of Shimmer, a prisoner somewhere. Why couldn't all those crows use their time and energy searching for the sacred object instead of gloating over the fact that such an important rook was on trial? They were probably all sitting around the Sacred Cliffs yearning for dawn so that they could witness the trial, for he know it would not take place between dusk and dawn. Once there is mob rule, thought Kos, out goes understanding, friendship and compassion.

From the peaty spongy bog a snipe rose in twisting flight across his path and vanished behind the rustling sedges. A badger trudged slowly across the land. As Kos got closer he saw that it was Bawson, his body squeezing and hissing water out of the black boggy soil as he waddled along. Kos was so pleased to see him on this grim night that he shrieked loudly. Bawson jumped at the blood-curdling shriek and went off rapidly through the dense mist in a panic, his whole body puffed out as he brushed over the purple moor grass.

'It's me, Kos . . .' Kos shouted after him.

There was a long silence.

Kos landed on a rock beside the badger, who was now lying among the sphagnum moss.

'You gave me a terrible fright,' said Bawson in scolding tones.

'Oh, I'm sorry,' replied Kos. 'But I was so pleased to see you,' he added.

'Oh, all right, then,' Bawson replied a little more calmly. 'It's good to see you. I keep thinking of Crag. It's hard to believe he's gone. I've been dreaming of him and he moves in the dreams but his legs don't move. It's crazy.'

'I was hoping I might find that magic Feather,' said Kos. 'I'd like to help Shimmer.'

'Good idea,' agreed Bawson. 'Maybe I can help. I believe the Feather will play an important part in all our lives, you know.'

Then the badger looked around and spoke in hushed tones, afraid someone or something might be listening. 'I came upon a very strange sight tonight, most strange indeed.' Kos listened intently. 'There's a place not far from here I'd heard of, but had never seen before tonight.

'It has tall standing stones and beside it is a cairn, an ancient burial place for the Nusham. It is said that trees which tried to grow near it died.

'My father once said that ghosts of the Nusham haunt the area, keeping guard in case anyone should trespass there. The sentinel stones are warnings. And the silence of death is all around the place.'

Bawson was trembling as he spoke. 'There are dry bones lying inside many underground chambers. Creatures have gone in and never come out.' He began to shake all over and told of seeing his worst nightmare come alive before his very eyes. 'Thousands of them, crawling, scurrying, twisting, clambering in and out of the shadows, then entering the secret burial chambers – down they poured, their squirming bodies wriggling. I've never seen so many in all my life, like the spawn of demons, their small feet and long tails scurrying over the damp earth – down they went into the secret passageways, down into the bowels of darkness.'

'Who?' asked Kos.

'Rats, that's who. Thousands, maybe millions of them, and mice and shrews and voles.' Then Bawson suddenly shouted: 'I've got it! That's it!'

'What?' Kos was puzzled.

'RATLAND! That's where RATLAND is. I remember hearing scary stories about it when I was a cub – a dangerous, evil place which was abandoned many, many harvest moons ago. Now it's being used again. This will bring a reign of terror, just you wait and see!' Bawson shook and shivered as if the icy hand of some ancient ghost had touched him.

'Calm down,' said Kos. 'It might only mean that rats have been evicted from some other place and gone there.'

'No,' said Bawson, 'it's more than that. I've had dreams, you see, frightening dreams!'

'Maybe this has something to do with the Sacred Feather? I'm going to find out, even if I have to go into RATLAND myself,' announced Kos.

'No!' said Bawson. 'It's too dangerous. They'd kill you. You wouldn't stand a chance against so many rats. Besides, you too have been in my dreams, surrounded by bloodthirsty rodents . . .'

Kos began to feel nervous, but then he thought of Shimmer and of how Shimmer had helped him when he was in danger. Kos vowed he would not fail, even if it meant dying in the process.

'I'll be all right,' said Kos, and he said farewell and flew off.

The moon could not pierce the thick, soft blue-grey mist and fog. Kos found it very strange flying through it. His own fear, and the chilly night air made him shiver. The very atmosphere seemed charged with terror. Wisps of mist rose like writhing phantoms.

Kos yelled a loud shriek in fear. He felt like turning back, but he had to go on. He must, he kept repeating to himself.

Soon he approached the dreaded place. A slender moonbeam revealed trees, their tortured forms casting weird, frightening shapes. Kos hesitated before the ominous stones which cast cheerless shadows on the ground.

The moon revealed the stones beside the entrance, with strange, swirling etchings carved deeply on them. Was this a warning to any uninvited creature who passed through? Kos alighted on the ground, then slowly and with extreme caution he went through the doorway.

Along the empty corridors he moved, brushing aside cobwebs, the musty, dank odour making him catch his breath. The splattered slime on the walls indicated the presence of black rats. Kos carried on down through the descending chambers. The sight of a Nusham skeleton crouched in a chamber set his heart pounding inside him.

His eyes darted at a movement up ahead. As he got closer he could see that the walls were crawling with earwigs, centipedes, lice and spiders. The entire passageway now reeked with the odour of rats.

On through another secret passageway he went, intense fear gripping him as he passed wall after wall of skulls. Their loathsome, frozen expressions repulsed him. Earwigs crawled through empty sockets; the silence of death lay all around. He had to stifle a terrible urge to shriek. He tried to shrug off these strange fears and set about finding the centre chamber. Another turn led him face-to-face with full-sized skeletons of owls, hawks and falcons.

Kos stumbled over a stone, knocking some skeletons to the floor and raising a cloud of choking dust. He flew in panic down the corridor. A yellow light flickered in the dreary blackness. Kos alighted on the floor and moved cautiously forward. He could hear laughter and merriment ringing loudly through the empty chambers.

Fearfully, he moved on, approaching the dangerous centre of RATLAND. Shadows of rodents danced like obscene blots on the chamber walls. The place was teeming with rats. Every space seemed to be occupied as they clambered over one another. An orgy of feasting was taking place.

Hack and Spike tossed a log on a blazing fire. Sparks jumped in the air momentarily, then vanished in the upper darkness. Fericul squatted on his throne, his eyes gleaming like burning coals. He was eating his favourite food – pigeon. Rats scurried around the large, carved standing-stone.

Spike called for silence, then turned to the Emperor. 'As a special tribute to our mighty leader, pray silence for the dance of the Rat King!'

The rats and mice moved aside to make room for seven rats who were all bound by their tails into a tangled, hairy knot. They moved around the floor and danced in unison. Their strange circular movement did look like a king's crown – hence the name, explained Spike.

'Very amusing,' remarked the Emperor. 'Bravo!'

Other rats performed various acrobatic feats to entertain the Emperor. Then, after they had all eaten and drunk their fill, they regaled each other with tales of conquests against the Nusham and other creatures.

Finally, Fericul gave a nod to Thrasher to indicate that he wished to speak.

'Silence for our leader!' roared Thrasher.

Kos watched from the safety of the shadows. He could see that this huge, black rat had a strange, terrible magnetism.

'My comrades,' said Fericul, 'everything is falling into place. My plans are being realised even as I speak. We now have our ancient home restored to us, by me.' Loud cheers from the rats, voles and mice. 'We will be conquerors of the earth. We are wise in the ways of cunning.' More cheers from the rodents. 'The Nusham fear, hate and persecute us. We have suffered imprisonment, torture, and have been killed in our thousands.'

His evil, red eyes darted in his head. Hack, Spike and Thrasher had heard the same words delivered many times by the Emperor, but they still sent shivers up their spines.

'We must take complete possession of the world,' Fericul continued.

'The Nusham live in a world of confusion, fear, wars, noise and smells. That suits us fine, my comrades. Their lives are distracted, and we can take advantage of that. Let us be the cunning adversary. We must sing a new song of hate. We will be reviled and feared. We will not be frozen, heated, decapitated, injected, drowned or eaten any more!'

Amid loud squeals of rage, the audience nibbled at each other's flanks and bit each others' tails in frenzied excitement.

'Once we have conquered the Nusham it will be easy to conquer the other creatures.'

'But how do you propose to do this?' a shrew asked timidly.

Fericul's red eyes glanced at the shrew, then a sinister smile broke over his face.

'I'm glad you asked me that, for that's why we are all here tonight. I promised you a gift and I will soon bestow it on you.' The Emperor signalled with his left arm and four rats came from another chamber carrying the gleaming Sacred Feather. Its light filled the room with a strange, mellow glow.

The rodents went down on all fours, noses to the ground.

Kos had never seen anything quite so beautiful as the Sacred Feather. Now he understood everything. The rats were going to get the gift of flight! They could then encompass all the earth and spread their terror wherever they went. It was too horrible to contemplate.

As Kos watched from behind some stones he noticed two shadows loom large on the wall. He turned his head – and there behind him were Whizzer and Skiter.

'Well, well, so we have a spy in our midst!' said Skiter with a sneer.

Kos froze with fear. He was trapped! The hoodies called to the Emperor.

'Look what was lurking behind the stones, Your Highness!'

All eyes were on Kos. The Emperor turned slowly towards him, and blazing eyes looked Kos up and down.

'Well, well, white owl. You are either very brave or very foolish to venture down here. My comrades, what will we do with one so foolhardy as to delve into our secret affairs?'

'Kill him!' shouted the mob of rats.

'That's taken for granted,' said Fericul. 'The question is, what way? Shall I pluck out all his feathers one by one? I believe that can be very painful. Perhaps tear his throat out? Or eat him alive? What do you think, my comrades?'

The rats and mice were silent, the Emperor's words making them shudder just to think about it.

'Still, he might be useful,' continued Fericul thoughtfully. 'Bind him and then we can kill him at our leisure!'

Hack and Spike wrapped ivy all around Kos and tied him to a large stone near the entrance.

Skiter and Whizzer then asked Fericul if he would like to hear about the trial of Shimmer, the old rook. The Emperor relaxed his menacing stance and sat up on his throne.

Skiter explained how the trial was led by a white-necked raven from Africa, for it was felt that the ravens who lived on the mountain were fond of Shimmer and might be too lenient with him.

'I've never seen so many rooks, carrion crows, hoodies, magpies and jays and all shouting "Death to Shimmer". It was very exciting indeed. There were also many who spoke highly of the old bird, but they were shouted down.'

The Emperor looked ecstatic. 'This will bring anarchy to the bird population; there will be division and doubt, bird against bird. It will be their downfall and our rising!' More loud cheers from the crowds.

'Yes,' he continued, 'we will soon be moving across the morning and evening skies better than eagle or falcon!'

Then Whizzer continued: 'The Council members said that Shimmer had recovered the Sacred Feather in the first place, after it had been lost for a very long time, and that he deserved credit for that. We pointed out that his having lost it again cancelled out his finding it in the first place.'

'You did well,' said Fericul. 'Continue.'

'Well, he was found guilty. The white-necked raven asked the crowd how he should be punished. Some said to bind his wings and throw him off the cliff; others said he should be allowed a chance to try and recover the Feather. Others shouted about starving him to death. We suggested pecking him to death, and the magpies thought our suggestion was the best. Finally, the Council suggested that his primary feathers be plucked from his wings, so that he wouldn't be able to fly – and if he could survive until they grew again he could go free.'

'Well, what happened?' asked Fericul, excited by it all. 'Is he wandering around somewhere, flapping his flightless wings? Tell me, so I can send out a couple of scouts and finish him off.'

'Well, unfortunately the trial was interrupted by a moth-eaten old owl called Barkwood. He claimed he had heard from reliable sources that the Feather had been stolen by hooded crows. This brought pandemonium as you can imagine. And he claimed that the Feather would be returned shortly and that friends of Shimmer were out looking for it at that very moment.'

Fericul did not look pleased. His mouth frothed as he asked who was looking for the Feather.

'A crazy old badger called Bawson,' Skiter answered nervously. 'And a young barn owl.'

The Emperor's stare transfixed Kos. 'A *barn owl*?'

All at once, Kos lost his fear. 'You will never be able to fly!' he shouted angrily. 'The Feather will not be used for evil!' Turning to the hoodies he said: 'You would betray your own kin for this power-crazy mob? Do you think they'll want you now that they have the

Feather? They won't! They're finished with you. Just wait and see.'

'Silence!' said the Emperor, and he moved slowly towards Kos.

'The magic can only be used on two days of the year – the summer solstice and the winter solstice,' continued Kos loudly. 'A beam of sunlight has to strike the Feather to release its full power. You'll never . . .'

'Why do you think I moved here?' yelled Fericul. 'Come winter, we will have the shaft of light we need.' He summoned Hack and Thrasher. 'Deal with this owl.'

Kos closed his eyes in horror as he felt Hack's nose touch his neck. Then a great noise erupted. An avalanche of foxes, owls, stoats, badgers and an otter spilled into the chamber, fangs and claws flashing. Hack and Thrasher disappeared in a flash.

'Attack, brave companions!' shouted Barkwood, who led the crowd.

The chamber was filled with screams and squeals as the brave friends battled with many thousands of rats. There were shrieks and hisses, and rats fell in their hundreds. The rescuers sent more scurrying up through the tunnels. Sheila, the heron, waited on the outside and picked them off as they passed through the chamber doorway.

'Attack!' yelled a furious Fericul, and rats clambered up on the foxes and bit deep into their chestnut fur.

Driad and Snowdrop were there too, and they stood near Kos while a small stoat bit through the ivy that bound him. Then he too was free to do battle. The three owls, joined by the offspring of Snowdrop and Driad, went into the fight together.

Rats leaped into the air and bit savagely at everything that came their way. Mice, shrews and voles scurried to the safety of different chambers. The owls raked the rats with their strong talons. The battle raged on and the chamber ran red with blood, the rats suffering heavy casualties. The fire was choked by falling dust from the ceiling.

Kos's friends were vastly outnumbered, but their greater size and individual strength and bravery, along with the surprise of the attack, helped them to win. The owls were deadly accurate with their violent air attacks through the smoke-filled room. This consolidated the ground attacks of the foxes, stoats, badgers and the otter.

Battle-weary rats scuttled away from the carnage, hordes of them escaping the dagger-bill of Sheila as they moved through her yellow legs out into the moving mist. The resistance collapsed, and the battle soon abated. The attackers had received many gashes and serious wounds, but no losses.

Kos and Driad had Fericul pinned down. He hissed and spat, but to no avail. His forces had fled. He had lost the battle, RATLAND, and the Sacred Feather. He squirmed in frustration and anger. Bawson sat on him while Kos and Driad searched for something to tie him up with. In one of the many chambers they found an old leather dog lead, evidently intended for the Emperor's prisoners. Fericul offered no resistance as they tied him, which made the badger uneasy, for he knew of the rat's terrible reputation. Clutching Fericul carefully, the victors, bruised and battered, made their way slowly out through the many corridors and tunnels.

There was a sudden cave-in which nearly trapped them all, but Bawson's strong paws dug them out. The walls of skulls had fallen and they had to make their way over a mound of skulls and bones. The upper corridors were strong, for they had been made by the Nusham with rocks and mud, and stayed standing.

Kos carried the Sacred Feather. He felt a strange but warm energy coming from it.

Barkwood was the first out into the fresh morning air, and they all followed, limping out slowly. The mammals threw themselves down on the short grass, exhausted, and the owls perched on the standing stones, preening and ruffling their delicate feathers to cleanse them of the dust and odour. Kos placed the Sacred Feather on the stone with the circles etched on it. It glowed like a fire and the light sent out its radiance, washing over them. They bathed in it, feeling the strength return to their aching bodies.

To their amazement all their wounds healed. The deep gashes across their eyes and down their flanks all disappeared like magic. Sheila moved in too to bathe in the mysterious light. She felt so good that her whole body relaxed as she crouched on one foot.

Kos thanked all his brave friends for making the perilous journey to RATLAND.

'Things have turned out wonderfully well,' said Bawson.

'All will be well in the woods again, just like old times,' declared Barkwood.

Fericul snarled. 'You may have won the battle because you caught us off guard, but the war is far from over. All the female rats will soon produce twice the litter to make up for our heavy losses. It's you who will be off-guard the next time. Then we will strike!

'I will personally train the black rats to have the will and power to grant us a swift victory. I will take immense pleasure in tearing out all your soft throats. I will inflict diseases that will wipe out anyone who gets in my way!'

His words brought a burst of anger from the younger animals. The otter wanted to kill him there and then, but Barkwood, who had assumed leadership called for calm.

'No, he must be brought to the Sacred Cliffs, to the

Council. Let them see what a vile creature he is and let them punish him rather than Shimmer.'

They took a vote on it, and it was unanimous. They would take him to the Council.

Sheila said it was time for her to leave. They all thanked her for her excellent efforts and she took off with a slow wing-beat. Neck tucked in and legs dangling, she headed into the mist, croaking a farewell as she vanished into the silvery grey light.

Suddenly, from behind, the two hoodies appeared at the doorway of the chamber and, quick as a flash, they flew over the heads of the owls who were perched on the stones. The owls watched them fleeing and they knew it would be pointless to try and catch them – the hoodies were too swift for that.

Barkwood recognised them as Shimmer's accusers and realised that it was they who had stolen the Feather. 'Those two are deadly enemies,' he announced to all the animals. 'They must be watched in future!'

Fericul was very pleased to see them escape. Watching their frantic flight, as they winged their way to safety, he knew they would not fail him.

Kos shrieked thanks to all the animals as he watched the otter, stoats, badgers and foxes leave. Driad and Snowdrop, pleased to have seen their young again, flew away promising to meet soon again.

Barkwood, Kos and Bawson sat silently, gathering their strength for the long journey to the Sacred Cliffs. They all felt that the great bond which already existed between them had strengthened as a result of the events in RATLAND.

'I didn't see any ghosts,' said Kos to Bawson, with amusement in his voice. Bawson gave a deep-throated laugh, then suddenly froze with fear, his eyes nearly popping from their sockets. He began to shake all over. Kos and Barkwood slowly turned their heads.

Out in the surrounding mist stood Crag. There was no mistaking his form. Like some ancient ghost he moved towards them, a dark shadowy figure in the gloomy light.

CHAPTER XIX

The Sacred Cliffs

Kos, Barkwood and Bawson could not believe their eyes. It really *was* Crag standing there beside them.

'Sorry I missed the fight,' he said, casually licking his fur. 'I believe it was very dramatic.'

Then he noticed the Sacred Feather. He padded over to it, stopped, sniffed the air gingerly, then circled it slowly.

'Beautiful!' he said. He sat in front of it as if in a trance, and the yellow hue covered his body as he gazed in wonder.

Kos flew to him. 'Is it really you, Crag, or is it a ghost?'

'No ghost, my little friend, it's me all right!' answered Crag.

'Well!' declared Kos, 'the last we heard, the hounds were upon you.'

Slowly, Crag moved over to sit beside Bawson, glancing at Fericul as he did so. 'Dear Bawson, I didn't know you were so attached to rats!'

This caused great merriment – and Fericul hissed like a snake.

'A nasty piece of work, if ever I saw one, Bawson. He's the one responsible for your nightmares, I should think,' said Crag.

'I had a dream of you moving across the land.'

'Listen, old pal, as I told you before, leave me out of your dreams!'

They all laughed again, but Kos persisted with his questions about the hounds.

'We thought you were dead,' he insisted.

'Dead lucky,' said Crag. 'I tried to make the hounds follow me. Some did. They chased me for a long time. I was exhausted, gasping my last breath. I slipped into a hedge and came out on a road. There was a car parked there and I jumped in the open window!

'The hounds were swarming around the car, barking and baying. Well, as luck would have it, two Nusham, a male and a female, who had been watching birds, hurried back to the car and drove off, leaving some very annoyed hounds behind.

'As we sped down that road I felt a mixture of relief and fear. Had I left one terrible situation to face another? I lay hidden under a mound of coats, trying to stifle my panting.

'They drove to a distant farm, not knowing I was in the back. The female kept sniffing the air as if she could smell me – when I get nervous I stink terribly.

'When we arrived at this farm the car stopped and the female turned to remove the coats I was hiding under. Then she saw me.

'I was worried but almost too exhausted to care. I stiffened back my ears and put on a threatening pose. I didn't know whether to bite or leap out the half-open window. I crouched – but she spoke to me softly.

'I didn't know what she was saying, but her tones were gentle and she had a pretty face, for a Nusham that is. Her chestnut-red curls cascaded down her face like a fountain and her eyes were kind. Her hands were gentle across my back as she removed grass and bits of thorn that had snagged my fur. Her long, caressing strokes down my fur made me feel very calm.

'The male was kindly too. He wrapped me in a blanket and carried me inside their home. Their two sheepdogs were none too pleased to see me and barked furiously. I clambered up over the male's shoulder.

'The Nusham held me firmly in his arms and the dogs were put outside in the farmyard. The female placed a small bowl with some food and water beside me. My paw was cut and the Nusham cleaned and bandaged it.

'Well, I experienced a dog's life for several days and I must admit, I enjoyed it. The dogs treated me with suspicion for a while, but they relaxed when we were all fed together.

'They quizzed me about living wild, the dangers, the woods. I told them all the woodlore I know. They loved to hear it and I think, in some ways, they were a little envious of my freedom. I then got the sad news about the death of my sweet Asrai. I will miss her terribly; she was a wonderful mate.' Crag's eyes misted over.

'She'll live on through your family,' said Kos.

'You're right, my little friend. I met them on the way over here; they told me all about what went on here.

'Well, when I was fit and well, the Nusham took me back to the spot where I had escaped the hounds. The Nusham female was sad to see me go – and the dogs licked me in friendship! The male Nusham lifted me into the field and they stayed until I trotted away. I stopped and yelped a "thank you", but I don't know if they understood.'

'I think the Feather saved you,' said Bawson. 'It truly is magic!' They looked at the Feather in awe.

Then Barkwood reminded them of Shimmer's plight and they set off on their journey to the Sacred Cliffs, Bawson pulling Fericul along on his leash. Crag held the Feather for part of the journey, then Barkwood and finally Kos carried it.

Kos was glad to get away from the burial site, although it did not look half as menacing in the daylight hours.

Crag was remarking on how suspicious of the Nusham he had always been, and yet he had actually been saved by two of them. 'Life never ceases to amaze me!' he added.

Barkwood flew up ahead, watching a flock of curlew beating windward across the bog. The morning was chilly as they made their way through the long grasses. Meadow pipits called in alarm; a stonechat clicked his message of annoyance from a gorse bush.

The going was slow and rough for Crag and Bawson. They knew they must hurry, for it was the season of brief days and long nights.

Fericul's skulking walk made Bawson nervous, for if the lead slackened between them he ran the risk of the rat springing up on him. The lead snagged several times on heather or gorse and turned into a tangled mess, with the help of the Emperor.

Finally, they came to wide, rolling fields and freshly ploughed earth. Crag stopped briefly to nibble a cluster of blackberries on a hedgerow. Bawson joined in. The two owls sailed silently out across the field, Barkwood holding the Feather with his feet. The fox and badger trotted after them, past oak trees hunched against the sky.

Another threat awaited the travellers. Lurking in a boggy hollow were Spike, Hack, Thrasher and a party of black rats. They watched the fox, badger and Fericul make their way over the damp fields. A blackbird called out a warning as the rats prepared to make their surprise attack.

Crag sniffed the gusting winds; something was up!

Then the rats sprang. Five of them leaped on Bawson, trying to release the Emperor. Bawson's sharp jaws bit back at the savage rats. The leather lead was bitten clean through, and Fericul, seizing his chance, scurried away, trailing the long lead that was still tied around his middle.

Crag was busy trying to stop the rats attacking his throat. Kos and Barkwood, hearing the commotion, turned quickly and flew back to help their friends. The owls pounced on the rats, piercing the life out of many of them. The marauding gang lay strewn on the grass, all dead except for Hack, Spike and Thrasher, who headed off after the Emperor. The fox and badger lay panting and exhausted.

Kos flew after Fericul and found him tangled in the lead with his legs partly bound. The others were trying to free him. Kos pounced on Thrasher, and Spike and Hack ran for cover. Fericul raged and wriggled to no avail. Kos jumped on the lead and held it firmly until the others came to help.

'What was that about missing the fight?' Kos said to Crag.

'I spoke too soon!' said Crag, amused. They managed to secure Fericul once more. This time Crag held the leather lead, locking it firmly in his jaws.

* * *

At the edge of the cliffs, Shimmer waited silently on a lichen-covered rock, totally isolated. The Council of Ravens sat in a semicircle around him. Would they carry out the punishment? Beyond this group were the birds who came to see, hear and jeer.

Shimmer was grateful to old Barkwood for speaking on his behalf, and persuading the Council to postpone punishment. He hoped the Feather could be recovered. He was not afraid to die, but he didn't want to die this way, bringing shame on his family and friends. He thought it strange that it should be an owl who would defend him, and another who had gone out searching for the Sacred Feather, when his own kind had turned against him.

The white-necked raven was anxious to have the case over and done with and his business completed, for the weather would soon change for the worse, and he was keen to return to Africa.

'We have waited long enough,' he shouted to the other council members. 'A serious crime has been

committed; the punishment is obvious. We can't sit around for days while some tired old owl and his companions search for the Sacred Feather. It's like looking for a twig in a forest – impossible!'

The crowds of birds yelled in agreement.

Granet, the oldest and wisest of the ravens, said: 'I hear what you say, my brother, but Shimmer has been a dear friend to us for a long time. I'm not anxious to hurt or destroy him . . .'

'It is he who will destroy us,' the African raven interrupted. 'With the loss of the Feather it's the end for us all. The winds of change are blowing across the world. If we're not shielded by the gift from the Eagle of Light we'll all perish. I've seen the signs in my own land.'

'My brother,' said Granet. 'Will the death of one rook stop the winds that blow so fiercely? But, very well. Justice must be done. We will give the owls until high noon. If they fail, we will proceed with the punishment.'

Thoughts of escape raced through Shimmer's mind, but he knew he would not get far. The peregrines who guarded the Sacred Cliffs would knock him from

the sky with their powerful yellow-clawed feet. No, if he were to die, he would not die a coward's death.

*   *   *

It was a long, arduous journey to the Sacred Cliffs; now they could see them towering up ahead. It was Kos's first time at the sea. Crag explained how the cliffs were shaped by the fury of the waves. A biting wind blew, stinging their eyes and wetting their fur and feathers. They were tired and hungry, but they knew it must not be far now.

Then they heard a piercing, harsh cry. They all froze. Into the stormy sky rose a magnificent falcon, cleaving the air. She was the embodiment of power and speed, her black streaks like a moustache against her white cheeks making her look very severe.

'Keep out, these are the Sacred Cliffs!' she called menacingly.

Barkwood replied that he had important business with the Council, a "matter of life and death", and he added that he had been there before and that the Council knew him.

The falcon then took off towards the plateau where the Council was sitting.

'So far so good!' said Crag, as they moved on. The wind was raw and blowing so hard that they found the going very difficult. Two hooded crows flew overhead – Whizzer and Skiter, hurrying to the cliffs too! Ahead, on a plateau, where the lichen rocks protected them from the force of the strong winds, sat thousands of crows and other birds.

All eyes watched the little group as they made their way up to the high point of the cliffs. A raven grunted. The peregrine sat on a lookout rock. And Shimmer's spirits rose, for he could see the Sacred Feather.

There was a great cheer as Kos placed the Sacred Feather on the ground between Shimmer and the Council. Their grim expressions softened to warm smiles. The Feather glowed, bringing a sense of calm to everybody. Each bird and creature was silent, staring at the precious object.

Then Granet, the raven, addressed them: 'Loyalty and friendship have returned the Sacred Feather to us. We can all breathe a sigh of relief.' Loud cheers came from the crowd. 'My dear friends, for your courage in risking your lives to save a friend and returning this most precious object, I hereby declare that your names will be written in the Book of Ravens, and you and your future families will always be welcome to the Sacred Cliffs.'

Kos, Barkwood, Crag and Bawson thanked him for the great honour. However, Crag in doing so had relaxed his hold on the lead. Fericul took his chance and scurried away, tearing Crag's mouth with the leather. Down the cliffs he went, with Kos in hot pursuit. The two hoodies flew after Kos as he flapped hard to catch the Emperor.

The Council did not know what was happening. They assumed the grey crows were flying to help Kos, but when they saw them knock the owl from the sky, sending him tumbling to the ground, they realised what was going on.

Crag raced down the slopes, followed by Barkwood. The two hoodies alighted on the ground. Whizzer fought with Kos, sending several quick stabs to his chest with his powerful beak, yet Kos kept a firm grip on him so he could not get airborne. Crag and Barkwood arrived and they quickly pinned the hoodie down.

Then, to everyone's amazement, Fericul clambered up on Skiter's back, with an anchor grip around his neck. The hoodie jumped from the cliff edge and flapped furiously across the sky. But it was slow going with the heavy weight. Crook-winged, Skiter hung in the air with Fericul holding on tightly.

'Faster!' the Emperor yelled as the hoodie used the

updraughts to float down along the edge of the cliffs. 'If we can make it back to the city dumps we will be safe. Faster!' yelled Fericul.

Bawson, meantime, had told the whole story of the rats' plan and how the hoodies had stolen the Feather. The white-necked raven called to the peregrine.

'They must not escape!' he said sharply.

The peregrine rose like a rocket into the clouded sky, higher and higher until she was nearly out of view. Her head swivelling, she scanned the cliffs with her binocular vision and spotted the evaders.

Arching her scythe-like wings, she dived, screaming loudly as she descended in corkscrew fashion through the sky. Fericul looked behind to see death-on-the-wing heading straight for him with yellow claws open wide, ready to strike.

Skiter and Fericul were torn from the sky – in an explosion of fur and feathers, they dropped like stones into the raging white waves. The triumphant screams of the peregrine told the Council and the others that her mission was completed. Moments later she was back on the plateau, preening herself.

Well, a trial did take place, but a hooded crow, not a rook, stood accused. Shimmer was restored to full honours and was to return as head of the rookery once more. He was also elected to the Council of Ravens, the first time any rook had received such a high honour. He asked for leniency for the hoodie as there had been enough bloodshed already, and, quoting from the Book of Ravens he said:

> 'In the great days of peace,
> all creatures will be one,
> as brothers and sisters living in harmony
> there will be no more killing,
> no claw, fang or tooth
> will be used against anyone of the Light.'

Whizzer launched himself into the air and flew away quickly. The other birds who had come to witness the trial dispersed slowly.

The Sacred Feather was carefully enshrined in a secret location, to be guarded by the Council members and the peregrines. Bawson, Crag, Kos and Barkwood stayed on for several days as guests of the ravens. They spent the time sharing stories and ideas, eating and resting. The white-necked raven was able to relate the most amazing tales about the vast continent of Africa, which pleased Kos greatly.

Finally, the time came for them to leave. The white-necked raven thanked them, and said that migrating birds would be forever indebted to them, now that their future was more secure because the Sacred Feather had been returned to the cliffs. Then he said his farewell to the Council, and began his long, arduous journey home to the distant continent.

Finally, Kos and his friends set off, to make the

journey home at last. Despite the cold, they all felt a warm inner glow. They did not speak, just moved on, looking at the different seabirds who had made their homes along the sheer cliffs – the fulmars, great black-backed gulls, kittiwakes, guillemots and razor-bills. They made their way through the great city under the protective cloak of darkness.

*　　*　　*

Not far away the rats had taken up residence again in the city dump. Whizzer sat with Hack and Spike, telling how the Emperor and Skiter had met their end by the yellow-legged falcon, how they plummeted to a watery grave. Hack and Spike had been convinced that the Emperor was invincible; but now that they knew he was dead they felt a sense of relief, for they could return to being normal rats again, instead of part of an army bent on the destruction of everything that was not a rodent. They sniffed the chilly night air, then scuttled down into their burrows. Whizzer flew off to find a warm roost.

*　　*　　*

The night had withdrawn and the sun was hanging like a lantern in the grey sky when the little group of friends finally arrived home. They passed by the big house which was near Shimmer's rookery. There was no need for words; they all knew their friendship was as powerful and as strong as the Sacred Cliffs themselves. Shimmer glided off like a black shadow across the bleak sky, to his colony.

'Well, as I said before, things are never dull with young Kos around!' said Crag to Bawson as they made their way across a grassy meadow towards the woods.

'Too true,' agreed the old badger.

Then Barkwood stretched his wings, shook his body, preened a little, and turned to Kos.

'But we're all very proud of you,' he said. Then, taking to the air, he fanned above the ground and flapped away silently.

Kos perched on the gatepost watching his friends depart. He sat in silent reflection. So many things had happened and he had learned so much. Probably the greatest thing he had discovered was that different creatures, with separate minds, could unite in one great purpose – through friendship.

Over the tangle of briar and hawthorn, Kos sailed in the silence of the morning across the barren fields. A light rain began to fall as he drifted slowly home.

CHAPTER XX

A New Visitor to the Woods

Kos emerged out of the dark recesses of the castle and alighted on the castle wall. It was a year to the day since he had taken his first flight from this wall into the unknown. He was glad to be back roosting again in the castle.

He had been surprised and delighted when Driad and Snowdrop had offered him the castle again. Snowdrop wanted to return to the area where she had been born. Kos enjoyed teasing Driad about going to live in a barn where the Nusham had put up special nesting-boxes for owls.

'It's warm, dry, roomy and safe,' Driad answered, 'and high up!' Driad and Snowdrop knew how much Kos loved Donadea Castle and were pleased to be able to return it to him. They were very proud to have

successfully reared a family there, especially with his help.

Kos was pleased too that all his friends were nearby. Bawson was like a young cub again since Crag had returned. And although he had not seen Barkwood recently, Kos knew that the old owl was out there, probably watching him right now, and would keep an eye on him for a long time to come. Crag, too, was very pleased to be living alongside Bawson's sett again.

Kos preened for some time, checking each feather very thoroughly. As he was about to go through the secondaries under his left wing, he noticed, out of the corner of his eye, a ghostly-white shape move across the darkened woods. Kos gave out an eerie shriek and took off to investigate, wafting low over the ground, past the mighty beech trees which looked even more impressive in their leafless splendour against the starry skies.

Three yelps from Crag told Kos that he was around somewhere, but Kos did not stop; he wanted to find the silver phantom. He searched in and around the woods without success. Had he imagined it? Was it a trick of the moonlight? Flying quietly over the muted fields, he searched for the elusive creature, landing on the gatepost where the trees stood sharp and clear against the star-curtained sky.

Kos sat silently hunched on the post, the moon bathing everything in silvery light. How could he find the mysterious creature? He was convinced it was a female owl. Maybe she could be a friend – or a mate? He had hardly seen her, but he was already en-chanted.

Then she appeared, greeting the moon with soft hisses like a lover. She gently folded her silvery wings, then alighted on the gate next to Kos. He trembled with excitement. He sat as if stunned, feeling uneasy, but elated. What would he say to her?

She preened her shoulder feathers; a fluffy white feather drifted into the midnight air. She seemed to glow in the moonlight. The two owls sat silent for a long time.

'You live here?' she asked finally, in gentle tones.

'Yes. Donadea Castle.'

'Beautiful,' she said. 'Is it good hunting country around here?'

'Yes,' said Kos.

'What is your name?' she inquired.

'Kos,' he answered. 'It's a very ancient name.'

'What does it mean?'

'Owl!' he answered. They both laughed. 'And yours?' he asked. He was beginning to relax now.

'Crannóg,' she replied. 'It's an ancient name too. My family lived on an island in the centre of a lake in Connemara. That's what my name means.'

'I like it,' said Kos. 'You know, I'm descended from a family of Galway owls too.' He asked her how she came to be in the woods of Kildare.

'Well, it's strange how it happened really,' she said. 'I was not long on the wing when I took my first long flight; my two brothers were still owlets. I was enjoying the freedom of my maiden flight, but was not as cautious as I should have been. I hit some wires and did a great deal of damage to my wing,' she said, indicating the right wing which had a slight droop in it.

'It's very difficult to see those black wires against a midnight sky,' Kos agreed.

Then she explained how she had lain on a road all night with her wing hanging loose. 'I was terrified. I was nearly flattened by the Nusham cars several times.'

'That's terrible,' replied Kos. 'Frightening!'

'One car stopped inches away from my body; the bright lights dazzled my eyes. Then a Nusham got out, picked me up and took me away in the car. It's faster than flying. I couldn't believe anything could move so fast, much faster than any hare!'

'Then what happened?' asked Kos.

'Well, the Nusham brought me to a place where there were lots of dogs, cats and birds in cages. I stayed there overnight. The next day a different Nusham fixed my wing and fed me, and I rested there for several days. I felt that these Nusham were friendly and were not going to hurt me. Did you ever get that feeling?'

'Oh, yes, several times,' replied Kos.

'One morning,' she continued, 'I was placed in a

dark box by the Nusham who had first found me. I was there for ages. Finally, after a long time, he opened the box and out I flew. It was dusk. I didn't know where I was, but my wing felt good and I knew there would be food to eat here and I would be safe unless the resident barn owls chased me off.'

'Oh, I wouldn't do that,' said Kos. 'I live alone; I'm glad of the company.'

'Have you no friends here?' Crannóg asked.

'Oh, yes,' replied Kos. 'Lots – a fox, a badger, a rook, a long-eared owl, a heron, an otter.'

'Really?' said Crannóg in surprise. 'You do have unusual friends!'

'Oh, you can meet them sometime, if you like. That is, if you would like to stay around these parts. Would you?'

She blinked her eyes gratefully. 'Will you show me around?'

Kos blinked back in pleasure. 'I'd love to. It would be wonderful!'

'Well, then, let's go!' said the silver owl.

And they flew away on silent wings.